Eric Kincaid

The best of
Fairy Tales and Fables

Illustrated by
Eric Kincaid

BRIMAX BOOKS · NEWMARKET · ENGLAND

Contents

© BRIMAX BOOKS LIMITED 1987. All rights reserved.
Published by BRIMAX BOOKS, Newmarket, England 1987
ISBN 0 86112 429 4
Printed in Hong Kong

THE TOWN MOUSE AND THE COUNTRY MOUSE

The Country Mouse watched sadly as his friend
the Town Mouse packed his bags to leave. The
Town Mouse had just spent a few unhappy days
at the Country Mouse's home under a hedge in a
field.

"You poor thing," said the Town Mouse with pity in his voice. "You
live so badly in the country, with only roots and corn to eat. Come back
with me to the town and I will show you what good living is like."

The two tiny creatures made the long journey to the house where the
Town Mouse lived, in the great city. At first, the Country Mouse thought
that life in the town was indeed wonderful. He had never seen such food
as there was in the larder. He had just started to nibble some of the dates
and figs stored there, when the door opened.

"Quick!" squealed the Town Mouse in a panic. "We must hide in my
hole!"

In an instant the Country Mouse found himself squashed against his friend in a small, dark hole. It was hot and very crowded.

After quite a long time, the Town Mouse said that it would be safe to leave the hole. The two animals came out into the larder, trying to stretch their cramped legs and shake the kinks from their tails. Still shaking with fright the Country Mouse picked up a fig again. Before he could eat it the door swung open again.

"Quick! Hide!" squealed the Town Mouse.

Yet again the Country Mouse found himself pressed against his friend in the tiny hole, with hardly room to twitch his whiskers, and with his heart beating wildly.

"That's it!" he told his friend firmly. "You may have very good food here, but what's the point of having good food if I'm always too frightened to eat it? I'm going back home."

So the Country Mouse packed his little bag and scurried back along the city streets until he reached his beloved fields again. With great contentment he crept back into his little hole under the hedge.

"This is the place for me," he said to himself, looking round at all the things he loved so much. "I like being able to twitch my whiskers and flick my tail whenever I want to. The Town Mouse can keep his old town!"

Moral: *Our own home always seems the best to us.*

THE FOX AND THE CROW

A hungry fox was prowling along looking in vain for food. It had been a long day and he was very hungry.

"What I would like more than anything else in the world," he said longingly to himself, "would be a nice piece of cheese."

Just as the thought passed through his head, the fox glanced up at the branches of a tree he was passing. To his amazement he saw a black crow sitting in the tree. In her beak was a piece of cheese. The fox licked his lips greedily. Somehow or other he had to get that cheese from the bird.

"Oh, Crow," he said admiringly, as if butter would not melt in his mouth, "what a beautiful bird you are to be sure. Your feathers are so soft and black, your beak so beautifully curved. If only – "

The fox stopped and shook his head doubtfully. The crow looked down, wondering what the fox was going to say next.

"If only," went on the fox, "your voice was as beautiful as your appearance, you would be a queen among birds."

Greatly flattered, the bird opened her beak and cawed loudly to show that she could sing. As she did so, the piece of cheese fell to the ground. The fox picked the cheese up and ran off with it.

Moral: *Beware of flattery, it may not be meant.*

ALADDIN

Once upon a time, there was a magician, who went to China to find a magic lamp he had heard about. He knew it was hidden in an underground cave, and he knew that the only way to get into the cave was through a narrow passage. He knew too, that if the clothes of anyone passing through the passage touched the walls, they would die. He didn't want to risk his own life, even for a magic lamp, so he made friends with a Chinese boy called Aladdin, and sent him into the cave.

"Wear this ring," said the magician as Aladdin got ready to climb down into the passage. "It may help to protect you."

"Protect me? Protect me from what?" asked Aladdin.

"Nothing," said the magician quickly. "There is nothing at all to be afraid of. Down you go, there's a good lad, and bring me the little lamp which you will find on a ledge at the back of the cave."

The Magician grew nervous, Aladdin seemed to be in the cave a very long time. He was just beginning to think Aladdin's clothes HAD touched the walls of the passage, and that he would never see him again, when he saw Aladdin's face framed in the gloom at the end of the passage.

"Have you got it? Give it to me!" said the magician eagerly. "Give me the lamp!" He reached down, and would have snatched the lamp from Aladdin, but Aladdin had put it in his sleeve and the magician could not reach it.

Aladdin had a feeling that perhaps the magician was not to be trusted, so he said, "Help me out first, then I will give you the lamp."

"Give me the lamp first," said the magician.

"Help me out first," said Aladdin. The magician wouldn't give in, and neither would Aladdin. Suddenly, the magician lost his patience and his temper.

"If you will not give me the lamp, then you can stay in the cave for EVER!" he shouted, and he closed the entrance to the passage with a short, sharp spell, and went away fuming.

Poor Aladdin! He didn't know what to do. He sat in the dark and tried to think. Then he absent-mindedly rubbed the ring which the magician had given him before he went into the cave. There was a hiss and a strange wispy figure, wearing a turban, curled up in the air in front of him like smoke from a fire. Aladdin gasped, and shielded his eyes from the sudden light.

"Who . . . who are you?" he asked.

"I am the genie of the ring. What is your command, oh master?"

"Can you take me home?" asked Aladdin.

Before Aladdin had time to blink he found himself standing outside his own house, wondering if he was asleep or awake. He knew he couldn't be dreaming, when he found the lamp tucked inside his sleeve. He took it to his mother.

"We can sell this and buy food," he said.

"No one will buy a dusty old lamp," said Aladdin's mother. "Let me clean it first." She had rubbed it but once, when there was a hiss, and another strange figure appeared and wavered in the air like a wisp of smoke.

Aladdin's mother was very frightened, but Aladdin asked, "Who are you?"

"I am the genie of the lamp. What is your command, oh master?"

And that's how it came about that Aladdin and his mother became rich. Whatever they wanted, the genie of the lamp provided, and when Aladdin fell in love with a princess he was rich enough to marry her and take her to live in a beautiful palace.

Aladdin and his princess lived happily for a long time. They shared all their secrets, except one. Aladdin never told the princess about the magic lamp.

One day, when Aladdin was out hunting, and the princess was at home in the palace, an old pedlar called from the street, "New lamps for old! New lamps for old!"

Now, although Aladdin had never spoken about the lamp to his princess, she had seen it, and when she heard the calls of the pedlar, who was really the wicked magician in disguise, she thought, 'I will get Aladdin a new lamp'. She ran into the street and exchanged, what she thought was a useless and broken lamp, for a bright and shining new one.

Immediately he had the magic lamp in his hand, the magician dropped the basket and threw off his disguise.

"Ha . . . ha . . . ha . . ." he chortled. "Now everything Aladdin has shall be mine." He summoned the genie of the lamp and ordered the genie to take him, Aladdin's palace and Aladdin's princess to far away Africa.

When Aladdin returned home there was nothing but dust and a bare patch where the palace had been. He guessed at once that the magician was responsible. He quickly summoned the genie of the ring.

"What is your command, oh master?" asked the genie.

"Please bring back my princess and my palace," said Aladdin.

"I cannot. Only the genie of the lamp can do that."

"Then take me to my princess, wherever she may be," commanded Aladdin.

That, the genie of the ring could do. And he did so. The princess was overjoyed to see Aladdin.

"I've come to take you home," said Aladdin. "But first we must outwit the magician and retrieve the lamp. Slip this powder into his wine when he is not looking."

The powder made the magician sleep, and while he slept Aladdin was able to take the lamp from his pocket.

Aladdin summoned the genie of the lamp.

"What is your command, oh master?" asked the genie.

"Leave the magician here in the middle of Africa, and take the palace, and everyone else in it, back to China," said Aladdin.

And that is what the genie of the lamp did. And everyone, except the magician, who woke up and found himself on a sand dune and who is still trying to work out how he got there, lived happily ever after.

THE CRAB AND HIS MOTHER

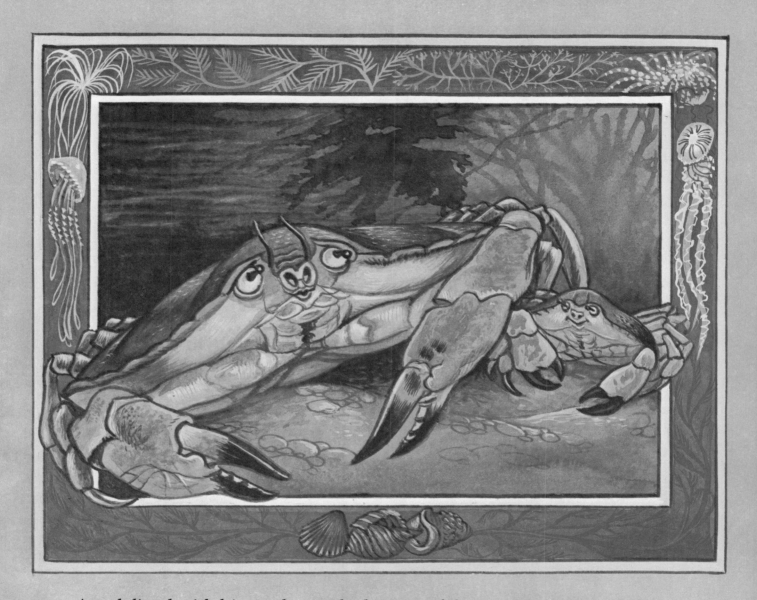

A crab lived with his mother at the bottom of the sea. The mother crab was very proud of her son, but she was always nagging at him to do better.

One morning she noticed her son scuttling across the sea-bed in the sideways motion that crabs have. "I wish you would walk forwards," she grumbled. "It would look much nicer."

"I will, mother, if you will show me how," replied her son.

The crab tried, but found that she could only walk sideways.

Moral: *We should not criticise people for what is not their fault.*

THE GREEDY FOX

It was the custom of a group of shepherds to hide their dinners in the shelter of a hollow tree before setting out to look after their sheep.

A clever fox saw what they did. For a number of days he hid, and watched the shepherds until he was sure that they did not come back to the tree for their food for some hours each day.

One morning, he watched the men hide their food as usual and then leave. The fox waited until the shepherds were out of sight and then he ran over to the hollow tree. The gap in the trunk was narrow, but by pulling in his sides he managed to squeeze inside.

Once he was in the tree the fox fell upon the food with a great appetite. He ate and he ate until he could eat no more.

Then the fox tried to squeeze himself out of the tree again. To his horror he found that he could not do so. He had eaten so much that his stomach had grown plump. No matter how hard he tried he could not squeeze in his sides enough to get out to freedom.

The trapped fox set up such a great howling that one of his friends heard him and came running over to the tree.

"Help me!" sobbed the fox inside the tree. "I have eaten so much that I have grown too fat to get out of this hole."

"There is only one thing you can do," said his friend, shaking his head.

"What's that?" demanded the fox in the tree hopefully.

"You will have to wait there until you grow thin enough to get out again," his friend told him bluntly.

Moral: *We should think before we act.*

THE HARE AND THE TORTOISE

A hare was a very fast runner, like most of his kind. He was always teasing a tortoise.

"You are so very slow," he would sigh as the tortoise ambled by. "I wouldn't be surprised if you were the slowest creature in the world. I don't suppose you even know how to hurry."

"Oh, I think I could move fast enough if I had to," said the tortoise happily, inching his way along.

The hare laughed. "What a funny idea," he jeered. "Why, I suppose you even think you could beat me in a race."

The tortoise stopped and thought. "Yes, I do," he said finally.

"Very well," the hare told him indignantly. "If you want to make a fool of yourself, we'll have a race."

The proposed contest aroused a great deal of interest among all the animals. On the day of the race they turned out in great numbers to see the fox start the two creatures off over the course he had arranged.

The hare set off at such a great pace that soon he had left the tortoise far behind and out of sight. Before long the winning post was looming up before the running hare. Suddenly an idea came to the animal and he skidded to a halt.

"I'll really rub it in," he said to himself. "I'll wait here until that poor tortoise comes into sight and then he can see me skip past the winning post."

With that idea in mind, the hare sat down under a tree for the time it would take for the tortoise to appear. It was a very hot day. Before long the hare had fallen asleep.

Meanwhile, the slow old tortoise had been plodding on doggedly. He passed the tree and the sleeping hare. Then he passed the winning post. The cheers of the watching animals woke the hare. To his amazement he saw that he had lost.

Moral: *Slow and steady can win the race.*

THE BEE-KEEPER AND THE BEES

There was once a bee-keeper who looked after a number of bee-hives together. We call such a collection of hives an apiary.

The bee-keeper kept his bees for their honey, but like all good bee-keepers he never took all the honey from the hives, but always left some for the bees.

One day a thief waited until the bee-keeper had gone off for his lunch and all the bees were out of the hives looking for pollen, from which they could make honey.

The thief was very greedy. He broke up the hives and took every scrap of honey that he could find. Then he ran off with it.

When the bee-keeper came back he saw what had happened. He was very upset.

"My poor bees!" he cried. "What will they do when they see their hives broken and all their honey stolen? I must try to put things right before they get back."

He set out to do this. He was just picking up the pieces of one of the broken hives when a swarm of bees returned. They saw all the damage and the broken honeycombs which had once held their honey. They also saw the bee-keeper standing over their ruined home. They thought that he must have destroyed it.

BZZZZZZZZZ   They were very angry. They attacked the poor bee-keeper and stung him again and again.

"It's not fair!" he shouted. "You let the man who stole your honey go free but you sting your friend and helper!"

Moral: *Things are not always what they seem.*

26

RAPUNZEL

One day, a Prince was riding in the forest when he heard a girl singing. He got down from his horse and led him quietly along a mossy footpath until he came to a clearing. In the clearing was a tower, as round and as straight as a giant pine tree. At the very top of the tower, which was so tall it looked as though its roof was touching the sky, there was a tiny window. It was from the tiny window that the sound of the voice was coming.

"It will be a long climb up the stairs to the top," said the Prince shading his eyes and looking upwards, "but I must find out who is singing so sweetly."

He looped the horse's bridle over a branch and went to look for a way in. He walked round the tower a hundred times. He could find no door . . . no window . . . no hidden entrance. It was impossible to climb up the outside for the sides were so smooth there was neither crack nor ledge where he could put his feet. In the end the disappointed Prince had to give up his quest and ride home with the sound of the voice drifting in the wind behind him.

The Prince could not forget
the voice. He dreamed about it
in daydreams and dreamed about it
in his sleep. He rode into the
forest every day, just to hear it.

One day, when he was sitting
in the branches of the tree
closest to the tower, an old witch
came out of the forest. The
Prince kept very quiet and
watched to see what she would do.

She went to the foot of the tower,
and called, "Rapunzel, Rapunzel,
let down your hair."

Immediately, a long braid of
golden hair tumbled from the
window at the top of the tower.
It was so long, its tip touched
the ground. The old witch caught
hold of it as though it was a rope
and someone, in the room at the
top of the tower, pulled her upwards
until she disappeared.

The Prince was so excited he
almost fell out of the tree. He
waited until the old witch had
come down again and hobbled away
into the forest, then he went to
the foot of the tower.

"Rapunzel, Rapunzel," he called. "Let down your hair."

Again the golden hair came tumbling from the tower, but this time it was a handsome prince who used it as a rope and not an ugly old witch. In the tiny room at the top of the tower was the most beautiful girl he had ever seen.

"Who . . . who . . . are you?" she gasped as he climbed over the windowsill and into the room. "I thought you were the witch."

"Do not be afraid," said the Prince, "I will not hurt you."

He told her his name and how he had heard her singing when he was riding in the forest.

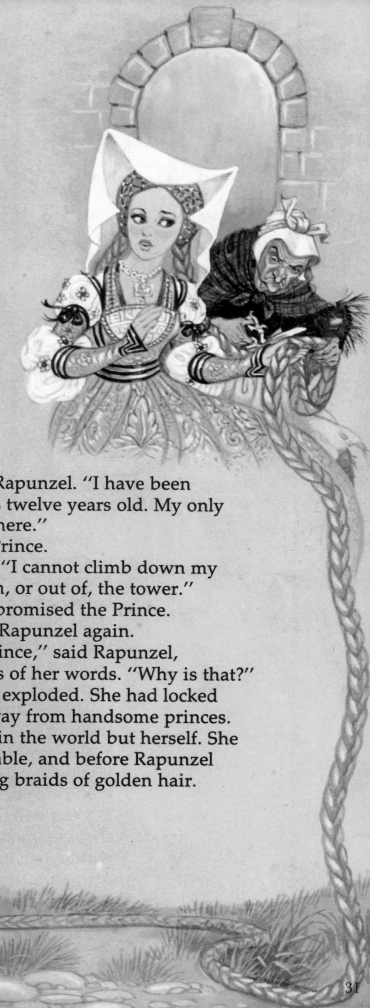

"I sing because I am lonely," said Rapunzel. "I have been locked alone in this tower since I was twelve years old. My only visitor is the witch who brought me here."

"I will help you escape," said the Prince.

"How can you?" sighed Rapunzel. "I cannot climb down my own hair and there is no other way in, or out of, the tower."

"I will bring you a silken ladder," promised the Prince.

That evening the old witch visited Rapunzel again.

"You are much heavier than the Prince," said Rapunzel, without thinking of the consequences of her words. "Why is that?"

The witch was so angry she almost exploded. She had locked Rapunzel in the tower to keep her away from handsome princes. She wanted Rapunzel to love no one in the world but herself. She snatched a pair of scissors from the table, and before Rapunzel could stop her she had cut off her long braids of golden hair.

"Now your Prince will never get into the tower," screamed the witch. And then, because she really was very angry indeed, she banished Rapunzel to a far-away place. Even if the Prince did find a way into the tower, Rapunzel would not be there.

The Prince had no way of knowing what had happened of course, and the next day, when he called to Rapunzel to let down her hair, he thought it was she who threw the long golden braids over the windowsill. But it was not. It was the witch. It was the witch who pulled the Prince upwards . . . and upwards . . . and upwards.

"You will never see Rapunzel again!" she screamed, as the Prince looked over the windowsill and straight into her ugly face. And with that terrible cry, she let go of the braids, so that they, and the Prince, fell to the ground.

The Prince was bumped and bruised, and when at last he stirred, and opened his eyes, he could not see. He was blind.

The Prince thought Rapunzel was locked in the tower with the witch and though he tried, he could find no way of helping her. He wandered about the countryside, blind, lonely and unhappy.

And then one day, just by chance, he came to the place where Rapunzel was living. He heard her singing and, though her voice was as sad as a flower without petals, he recognized it at once.

"Rapunzel," he called softly. "Is that you?"

Rapunzel was overjoyed, but when she saw the Prince's poor blind eyes, she wept hot, splashing tears. Some of her tears fell onto the Prince's face. Suddenly he could see. Her tears had broken the witch's terrible spell.

Rapunzel and the Prince were married and lived happily ever after. And as for the old witch, she was never heard of, or seen again. Perhaps she is still locked in the tower. Once she had let go of the braids she had no way of getting out of the tower herself, had she?

A WOLF IN SHEEPS CLOTHING

"There are dozens of sheep in that flock down there," said a wicked old wolf to himself, gazing down at a field. "How can I get close to them so that I can kill and eat some?"

Then he had an idea. He found an old sheepskin and wrapped himself up in it, so that he looked like a sheep. Then he walked down to the field and joined the flock of sheep grazing there.

The sheep thought that the wolf was one of them, so they paid no attention to him as he moved among them. Not even the shepherd noticed who the wolf really was.

The wolf decided that it would be best to wait until dark before he fell on the fattest sheep and ate it. By that time the shepherd would have gone home.

When the sun went down behind the distant hills, the shepherd drove his sheep and the wolf in the old sheepskin into the pen which gave them shelter at night. Then he went off to his cottage to sleep.

The wolf had just decided which sheep he was going to leap upon, when suddenly the door of the pen was thrown open. A farmer stood in the doorway.

"We want some fresh meat at the farmhouse," he said. "One of you sheep will do. Yes, you over there! You look a big fellow."

With that, the farmer lifted his axe and brought it crashing down on the wolf, thinking that he was a sheep.

Moral: *Sometimes we can be too clever for our own good.*

THE NORTH WIND AND THE SUN

The North Wind and the Sun met far above the earth and had a great argument.

"I am stronger than you!" roared the North Wind.

"Oh no, you're not!" smiled the Sun happily.

For weeks their argument raged. Neither the Sun nor the North Wind would give way. They became so wrapped up in their dispute that they ignored their jobs. The North Wind did not blow, and the Sun would not shine.

In the end they decided that they must settle their argument once and for all, before something dreadful happened to the weather on earth.

In the end they agreed that the first of them to separate a certain traveller from his cloak could consider himself the stronger of the two.

The North Wind tried first. He leapt upon the poor traveller, roaring and blowing. He tried his hardest to tear the cloak from the man's body. He failed. All that he did was to make the windswept man hug his cloak closer to him for protection.

"It's impossible," groaned the North Wind, retiring and leaving the traveller to continue on his way. "If I can't separate that man from his cloak with all my strength, I'm sure that you won't be able to, Sun."

The Sun did not answer the surly North Wind. He merely carried on smiling. He smiled down on the traveller below him. His smile began to make the traveller feel warm. Before long, the man stopped hugging his cloak to him and let it fall open. The Sun's smile grew warmer and warmer. The traveller threw his cloak back behind him, so that it hung from his shoulders. Still the Sun smiled. The earth grew warmer and warmer. Everything began to wilt and droop in the enormous heat. In the end, the traveller knew that he did not need his cloak at all. He took it off and trailed it in the dust behind him.

The Sun turned to the North Wind. He still said nothing, but his smile grew even wider.

Moral: *It is sometimes possible to gain by persuasion what cannot be gained by force.*

TWELVE
DANCING PRINCESSES

Once upon a time, there was a King who had twelve beautiful daughters, and an unusual problem. Every night, when the twelve princesses were sent to bed their shoes were perfectly sound. Every morning when they came down to breakfast their shoes were full of holes. Every day the King had to buy twelve pairs of new shoes. That was expensive, though the expense did not worry the King. What did worry him was not knowing WHY the shoes were full of holes.

He tried locking the bedroom door on the outside when all the princesses were safely inside, and sleeping with the key under his pillow. It made no difference. The princesses' shoes were still full of holes in the morning.

The King was so puzzled, and so vexed, because he couldn't find out WHY it was happening that he issued a proclamation.

It said, WHOMSOEVER SHALL DISCOVER WHY THE PRINCESSES' SHOES ARE FULL OF HOLES EVERY MORNING SHALL HAVE ONE OF THE PRINCESSES FOR HIS WIFE AND SHALL INHERIT MY KINGDOM WHEN I DIE.

Princes came from far and wide to try to find an answer to the mystery. Not one of them succeeded. The puzzled King was beginning to despair of ever finding an answer when a poor soldier came to the palace. The proclamation had said nothing about being a prince if you wanted to solve the mystery, so he had decided to make an attempt at it himself.

The King received the soldier as kindly, and as grandly, as any of the princes, and that night he was taken to a room adjoining the princesses' bedroom so that he could keep watch.

Now it so happened, that the soldier had been kind to a wise old woman on his way to the palace, and she had given him a cloak, and some advice. "When the princesses offer you wine," she had said, "pretend to drink it and then pretend to fall asleep. Wear the cloak when you want to be invisible."

That night, when the princesses were ready for bed, the eldest said to the soldier, "You must be thirsty. Take this cup of wine and drink."

The soldier remembered the wise woman's words and pretended to drink. And then, he pretended to get drowsy. Presently he closed his eyes as though he was asleep.

As soon as they heard him snore the princesses jumped from their beds and put on their shoes and their prettiest dresses.

"Are you all ready?" asked the eldest.

"We are ready," replied her sisters.

The eldest princess pressed a carved leaf on the end of her bed. The bed moved slowly to one side and revealed a hidden staircase leading down into the earth. The princesses picked up their skirts and hurried down the steps, the eldest leading the way, and the youngest following last of all.

The soldier, who of course was awake and had seen everything, put the cloak the old woman had given him round his shoulders. It covered him from head to toe and made him completely invisible.

He ran after the princesses and caught up with them at the bottom of the steps. He was in such a hurry not to be left behind that he accidentally stepped on the hem of the youngest princess's dress, and tore it.

"Oh . . ." she gasped. "Someone has stepped on my dress."

"Don't be silly," said her sisters. "You caught it on a nail . . . come hurry . . . we must not be late."

At the bottom of the steps there was a wood in which all the trees had silver leaves. The soldier broke off one, and put it in his pocket.

"What was that?" cried the youngest princess in alarm, as she heard the snap of the breaking twig.

"It was nothing . . ." said her sisters.

Next, they passed through an avenue in which all the trees had golden leaves. Again the princess heard the snap of a breaking twig, but again her sisters told her it was her own imagination playing tricks on her.

The running princesses came to the shore of a wide blue lake. At the edge of the lake were twelve boats, and in the boats twelve handsome princes were sitting, waiting, at the oars. The soldier sat in the boat which was to carry the youngest princess.

"I wonder what makes the boat so heavy today," said the prince, as he pulled, harder than usual, at the oars.

On the far side of the lake there was a magnificent palace from which the sounds of music and merry-making came . . . and it was there that the mystery of the worn out shoes was solved. The twelve princesses danced the entire night with the twelve handsome princes.

Just before dawn, and when all their shoes were in shreds, the princes rowed the princesses back across the lake, and the princesses ran home.

As soon as they reached their bedroom they hurried to look at the soldier. He had run home ahead of them and they found him on his bed, still sleeping, or so they thought.

"We are safe . . ." said the eldest princess.

The soldier followed the princesses to the secret palace the next night, and the following night too. On the third night he took the jewelled cup from which the youngest princess drank and slipped it into a pocket in the invisible cloak.

On the morning after the third night, the King sent for the soldier, and said, "Your time is up. Either tell me why my daughters' shoes are worn through every morning, or be banished forever . . ."

"Your daughters' shoes are worn because they dance every night in an underground palace," said the soldier, and he told the King all that he had seen.

The princesses gasped and turned pale as the soldier took the silver leaf, the golden leaf, and the jewelled cup from his pocket and handed them to the King. They knew now they could not deny that what the soldier said was true.

"We must confess," said the eldest princess.

The King was so relieved to have the mystery of the worn out shoes explained, that he couldn't stay cross with his daughters for long.

"Now I shall be able to sleep at night," he said.

The King kept the promise he had made in the proclamation, and the soldier married the princess of his choice. And many years later, when the old King died, the soldier became King in his place.

THE HOUND AND THE HARE

A hare was playing happily on her own in a field when suddenly a hound came bounding up to her. The hare squealed with terror, thinking that her end had come. The great dog snapped at her with fierce teeth. The hare closed her eyes, expecting the worst. To her surprise, the dog did not bite her. Instead he stopped snarling and snapping. The hare opened her eyes and peered at the hound.

"Come and play with me," invited the dog, wagging his tail.
"Certainly not," snapped the hare. "I wouldn't dream of it."
"Why not?" asked the disappointed hound.
"Because I don't know what to make of you," replied the hare. "If you are my friend why do you try to bite me, and if you are my enemy why do you want to play with me?"

Moral: *We like other people to show themselves to us as they really are.*

THE MOON AND HER MOTHER

The moon was so beautiful that she became vain and wanted to look even lovelier. She asked her mother to make her a gown that she could wear as she drifted lazily across the sky. To her surprise her mother shook her head sadly.

"Alas, that is something I can never do for you," she said.

"But why not?" cried the moon, greatly disappointed. At that moment, she wanted a gown more than anything else in the whole world.

"Think for a while," advised her mother, "and then you will see that I could never make a gown that would fit you."

"But why not?" the moon sobbed.

"Because you are always changing," her mother told her. "At times you are so thin you can slide under a closed door. Yet at other times you are so full and round, people could easily take you for a cheese. And between these two sizes, you are neither thin nor fat, but all different shapes."

Moral: *Someone who is always changing cannot expect others to regard him as one particular thing.*

THE QUACK FROG

A frog grew bored with living by the banks of a pool and croaking all day long. He decided to move to the town and make his fortune. In order to do this, he thought he would set up in the market place there as a quack doctor. This is not a real doctor but a false one who claims to be able to cure anything.

So the frog hopped into the market-place and set up a stall there. He filled the counter of this stall with all sorts and sizes of bottles. He had green bottles, blue bottles, brown bottles and clear ones.

When he was ready he climbed on to a box, so that all could see him, and began to shout.

"Roll up! Roll up!" he cried. "Come to me with all that ails you, and I promise to cure you of all illnesses!"

A great crowd of animals, attracted by this rash promise, began to gather about the frog's stall. Among the onlookers was a fox.

"Are you sure that you can cure anything?" asked the fox.

"Of course," lied the frog. "I have studied with all the most famous doctors in the world. The contents of my bottles here can cure all ailments."

At these words the animals began to press forward, buying the bottles from the frog at a great rate. But the clever fox was not satisfied. After looking on for some time he asked quietly:

"If you are such a clever doctor, how is it that you cannot walk, only jump? And why is your skin so blotchy and wrinkled?"

There was no answer to this. The crowd of animals began to shout and jeer and demand their money back. The frog was forced to hop away from the town back to his pool.

Moral: *Physician heal yourself*.

48

THE SWAN AND THE CROW

There was once a black crow who wanted to be a white swan. This crow lived in a tree, like all other crows. He led a perfectly happy life, with a strong nest to live in and good food to eat, but he was not content. He saw the graceful swans beating their way through the air with their strong wings and sailing proudly on rivers, and wanted to be just like one of them.

"I wish my wings and body were white like the swans are," he said to himself. "Why can't I be like a swan? It's just a case of trying hard enough."

So the crow decided to turn himself into a swan. First he went to live by the side of a river, as the swans did, leaving his warm nest in the tree. For weeks he watched the swans as they floated on the water and flew into the sky, trying to remember everything that they did. Then he set out to copy them in every detail.

He taught himself to swim in the flowing water. Each day he scrubbed away at his black feathers, trying to make them white. He ate the same food as the swans.

Nothing worked. The crow's body remained black. The swans' food did not agree with him and he grew thin. The water made his wings weak and bedraggled.

In the end, the crow realised that he was never going to turn himself into a swan. The knowledge disappointed him so much that he flew away from the river and died.

Moral: *We may change our habits, but we cannot change our nature.*

50

51

THE THREE SPINNERS

Once there was a girl who could not spin thread. She could do other things, but she could not, or would not, spin. It made her mother very angry to see her sitting idle at the spinning wheel.

"You lazy, lazy girl," she would shout, and then she would hit the girl across the shoulders.

One day, when she was shouting, and the girl was sitting crying at the spinning wheel, the Queen happened to pass by in her coach. She heard the girl crying and called to her coachman to stop the horses.

"Why are you beating your daughter?" she asked. "Why are you shouting at her? Why is she crying? What has she done?"

A Queen's questions should always be answered truthfully, but the old woman was too ashamed to say she thought her daughter was lazy, so she said instead, "My daughter loves to spin. I am only a poor old woman and I cannot afford to buy the flax. She cries because she wants to spin . . . I do not know what to do."

"Your troubles are over," said the Queen, who as it happened, loved to hear the whirr of the spinning wheel and to see freshly spun thread. "I have plenty of flax at the palace. I will take your daughter home with me and she can spin as much as she likes."

The Queen took the girl to the palace and showed her three rooms which were full from floor to ceiling with unspun flax.

"Spin all THAT flax into thread, my dear, and you shall marry my son," said the Queen.

The poor girl did not know what to do. Of course she wanted to marry the Prince, but how could she? She didn't know HOW to spin. For three whole days she sat and wept. On the third day the Queen came to see her.

"Why are you weeping child? Why haven't you started to spin?" asked the Queen.

The poor girl sobbed even harder.

"I brought you to the palace to spin flax," said the Queen sternly. "If there is no thread for me to see tomorrow you will be punished."

When the Queen had swept majestically from the room, the poor, sad girl stood at the window overlooking the street and cried as though her heart would break. Presently, through her tears, she saw three strange women walking along the pavement. One of them had a very broad, flat foot. One had a lip that hung down over her chin, and the third had an enormous thumb.

One of the women called up to the window and asked the girl why she was weeping.

"I do so want to marry the Prince," she sobbed, "but first I must spin all this flax, and I do not know how to spin."

"If you will call us aunt and be unashamed of our strange appearance, and if you will invite us to sit with you at your wedding, we will help you," said the three women.

"I shall be glad to call you aunt," said the girl.

The three strange women were as good as their word. They slipped unnoticed into the palace and set to work. The one with the broad, flat foot worked the spinning wheel. The one with the lip which hung over her chin wetted the flax. And the one with the enormous thumb twisted the thread. Together they spun the finest thread the Queen had ever seen. She was impressed, though she thought the girl herself had done the spinning for the three stange women hid whenever they heard the Queen coming.

At last all the flax had been spun and it was time for the wedding. When the arrangements were being made, the girl said to the Queen, "I have three aunts who have been very kind to me. May I invite them to the wedding and may they sit with me at the table?"

"Of course," said the Queen.

An invitation was sent, and on the day of the wedding the three strange women arrived and were welcomed kindly by the girl and the Prince.

"Tell me Aunt," said the Prince, who couldn't help noticing such things, "why have you such a broad flat foot?"

"Because I tread a spinning wheel," said the first aunt.

"And how is it that you have such a long lip?" he asked the second aunt.

"Because I wet the spinning thread."

"And why have you such a large thumb?" asked the Prince of the third aunt.

"Because I twist the spinning thread," she answered.

The Prince looked at the three strange women, one with a broad flat foot, one with a lip that hung down over her chin and one with an enormous thumb, and then he looked at his beautiful bride.

"If that is what spinning thread does to a woman," he said, "I forbid you to touch a spinning wheel ever again."

And so the girl married her prince, and the three spinners moved into the palace to take care of all the spinning. They loved spinning as much as the girl loved the Prince and so everyone was happy.

THE LAMP

The lamp was very proud of itself. It was polished and very beautiful. When it was filled with oil and lit, it shone so brightly, casting a soft, glowing light over the room it was in.

"Just look at me," said the lamp proudly. "I really am a most wonderful lamp. I give as much light as the silver moon in the sky. I shine as beautifully as the moon and all the stars in the heavens put together. More than that, I really believe that I shine as brightly as the great sun itself."

At that moment a great gust of wind blew into the room through the open window. The wind was so strong that it blew the light of the lamp out altogether. The room was plunged into darkness.

"Now do you see how foolish you are?" asked the lamp's owner as he relit the lamp. "How dare you compare yourself with the sun, moon and stars. They all cast their light for ever, while a mere puff of wind can put you out!"

Moral: *Pride comes before a fall.*

THE PEACOCK AND THE CRANE

Once there was a peacock who was very proud and vain. He boasted to everyone about his beautiful feathers. If it rained, he would stand looking at his reflection in puddles.

"Just look at my tail!" he would crow. "Look at the colours of my feathers. I am so beautiful! I must be the most beautiful bird in the world!"

At this he would open his tail like a great fan and stand waiting for someone to come along and admire him.

The other birds became annoyed at the boasts of the proud peacock and tried to think of a way of taking him down a peg. It was the great bird called the crane who had an idea.

"Leave it to me," he told the others. "I'll make that vain peacock look foolish."

One morning the crane strolled past the peacock. As usual the peacock was preening his feathers.

"Am I not beautiful!" he cried. "You are so plain and dull, Crane. Why don't you try to look a little smarter?"

"Your feathers may be more beautiful than mine," said the crane calmly. "But I notice that you cannot fly. Your beautiful feathers are not strong enough to lift you from the ground. I may be dull, but my wings can carry me into the sky!"

Moral: *We may lose in one way, but gain in another.*

THE MICE AND THE WEASELS

For months the weasels and the mice had been at war. The weasels were bigger and stronger than the mice, they won battle after battle. The surviving mice called a meeting.

"I have a plan," said one mouse. "We have lost all our battles because we do not have any leaders. I vote that we choose four mice to be our generals and lead us into battle."

The other mice agreed that this was a good idea. They chose four of their number to be generals and lead them in the war. To show that they were generals, the four mice were given large helmets with great feathers called plumes in them. They also had large heavy badges dangling on ribbons from their necks.

Before long, the four generals began to feel very important. They held many meetings at which they made plans to defeat the weasels. They talked so bravely it made them feel proud and strong.

When they felt that they were ready, they led the other mice into battle. Alas, for all their plans they were still defeated. After a fierce battle the mice turned and fled.

Most of the mice reached their holes and were safe. The four generals ran too, but they were so weighed down by their plumed helmets and badges that they were the last to reach their holes. When they did, their helmets and badges were so big and heavy, they could not get in quickly enough. The weasels caught up with the poor generals and fell upon them.

Moral: *Vanity is foolishness*.

THE TRAVELLER AND HIS DOG

A man was about to set out on a long journey. He was rather fussy and wanted everything to be just right. In order to make sure that this was so, he spent days getting ready. He tidied everything up in his house and prepared a great deal of food for the trip.

When he was quite ready, he put on his travelling clothes and put his pack on his back. Only then did he leave his house. His faithful dog was waiting for him outside.

"Why are you sitting there, doing nothing?" grumbled his owner. "Do I have to do everything? Come on, get ready to come with me."

The dog wagged his tail politely.

"But I am ready, Master," he said. "*I* have been waiting for *you!*"

Moral: *We tend to blame others for our own mistakes.*

THE EMPEROR'S NEW CLOTHES

Once there was an Emperor who was always changing his clothes.
He had a different outfit for every hour of the day. Whenever
his ministers wanted him for something special, they always went
to the royal clothes closet first. He was more likely to be there
deciding what to change into next, than passing laws in his
Council Chamber, or balancing the budget in his Counting House.

One day, two men arrived in town. They knew how fond the Emperor was of new clothes and they had hatched a plan. A crafty plan. They spread the news that they could weave the most beautiful cloth anyone had ever seen, and furthermore it was magic, and invisible to anyone who was stupid, or unworthy of the position they held.

"I must have an outfit made from that marvellous new cloth everyone is talking about," said the Emperor, and he sent for the weavers. They agreed to weave some of the cloth for him and went away from the palace carrying silk and golden thread, as well as a large sum of money.

They hid the silk and golden thread in their packs and then set up their loom. There was the steady clack, clack, and the whirr of a busy loom for days. The Emperor was very anxious to see how the new cloth was coming along, but he was just a tiny bit afraid.

'What would I do if I could not see the cloth?' he thought. And though he didn't think for a moment that he wasn't fit to be emperor, he sent his faithful old Prime Minister to look at the cloth in his place.

The weavers led the Prime Minister to their loom. He could not see a single thread.

'Oh dear,' he thought, 'if the Emperor finds out I can't see the cloth I will lose my job. I must pretend I CAN see it.'

"It's the most beautiful piece of cloth in the world," he told the Emperor on his return to the palace.

The Emperor decided perhaps he would go and see it for himself after all. He gathered his favourite councillors around him and went to the weavers.

"Show us our beautiful new cloth," he said.

"Can you not see it? It's there, on the loom," said the weavers.

"So it is . . . so it is . . ." said the Emperor, his voice full of admiration and his heart full of shame, because HE could not see the cloth either. But then neither could anyone else, though everyone THOUGHT everyone else could see it. There were so many exclamations of delight at the beauty of the new cloth, it really was quite astonishing, in the circumstances.

"Make me a suit of clothes from the cloth and I will wear it in the procession tomorrow," said the Emperor, outwardly smiling, and inwardly trembling.

The two weavers said they were tailors too, and that they would make the suit themselves. At eight o'clock next morning it was ready. Or so they told the Emperor.

The Emperor bathed. He powdered his hair. He put on his shoes and stockings. And then he let the weavers dress him in the new suit of clothes.

"It's a perfect fit," they said.

"It's a perfect fit," said ALL the councillors.

"It's a perfect fit," said the Emperor, although he could see nothing but his own pink skin.

When the Emperor was ready, or thought he was, the procession through the streets of the town began. Everyone knew about the wonderful cloth. Everyone knew that only those worthy enough could see it, and that to everyone else it was invisible.

"Look at the Emperor's new suit . . .isn't it beautiful . . .?" sighed the people in the crowd as he walked proudly by.

"How well it fits . . ."

"Ahhh . . . truly a suit fit for an emperor . . ."

And then a little voice rang out above the others. It belonged to a boy who never listened to gossip and he hadn't heard the stories about the wonderful cloth, besides his father had taught him always to be truthful.

"The Emperor has no clothes on!" he shouted.

Someone began to laugh. "The boy is right! The Emperor has no clothes on!"

The cry was caught up by the people in the crowd.

"The Emperor has no clothes on . . ."

The poor Emperor was shivering with cold so he knew the crowd must be right, but he walked proudly through the streets and back to the palace with his head held high and his skin blushing a bright and glowing pink.

He sent guards to fetch the weavers so that they could be punished for daring to trick an emperor, but they had vanished and were never seen again. And from that day onwards, I'm glad to say, the Emperor paid a little less attention to what he wore, and more attention to the affairs of state.

THE WOLF AND THE GOAT

A cunning wolf saw a goat nibbling grass at the top of a hill.

"What a good dinner you would make," said the wolf to himself, licking his lips hungrily.

He walked forward and gazed longingly up at the goat. He was not nearly as sure-footed as the other animal. There was no way in which he could climb the cliff and fall upon the goat. Somehow he had to persuade the goat to come down to him.

"Good morning, Madam Goat," he called out, putting on his most engaging smile. "Pray take a care. It is so dangerously high on that cliff. I should hate you to come to any harm. I'll tell you what! Why don't you come down here, where the grass is fresh and green. I speak to you as a friend."

The goat was not to be fooled. She looked down at the wolf and shook her head.

"You can't trick me," she called down. "You don't care whether the grass I eat is fresh and green, or dry and brown. All that you want to do is to eat me!"

Moral: *Look before you leap.*

THE EAGLE AND THE BEETLE

The eagle and a tiny beetle fell out with one another and became deadly enemies.

It happened in this fashion. One day the eagle was chasing a hare across a field. It swooped low over the terrified animal, its great claws extended, its beak ready to strike.

The poor hare ran as fast as it could, screaming for help. The only living thing it could see was the tiny beetle.

"Help me, beetle! Please help me!" cried the hare piteously.

The beetle was small but brave. "Eagle!" he cried in his loudest voice. "I am speaking to you, eagle! Do not touch that hare. It is under my special protection!"

Of course, the eagle took no notice at all. In fact he hardly noticed the tiny beetle. Suddenly he pounced upon the hare and ate it.

The beetle was very upset about this and decided to avenge the hare.

He made his way to the eagle's nest, high in the cliffs, and waited. Then, every time that the eagle laid an egg, the beetle rolled it out of the nest, so that it fell to the ground below and was smashed.

The beetle destroyed so many eggs in this way that the worried eagle went to the god Jupiter, and asked his advice.

"You may lay your eggs in my lap," said the god. "They will be safe there. The beetle will not dare approach me."

But Jupiter did not know how determined the tiny beetle was. When he started something, the beetle always did his best to finish it. He waited until the eagle had laid a clutch of eggs in the god's lap. Then he rolled a lump of earth into Jupiter's lap.

When the god saw the dirt on his lap he stood up quickly and brushed it off. But he had forgotten that the eagle's eggs were also on his lap. As he stood up, these fell to the ground and were smashed. The beetle had won again!

Since that day, or so it is said, eagles have always made sure that their eggs are laid in a safe place, which is why people hardly ever see them.

Moral: *Great determination can overcome most odds.*

PUSS IN BOOTS

Once upon a time, there was a miller, who had three sons. When he died he left his mill to his first son, his donkey to his second son, and because he had nothing else, he left his cat to his third son.

The first son ground flour at the mill and sold it. The second son harnessed the donkey to a cart and carried things for paying customers. But what could the third son do with a cat, except let him sit in the sun, and purr, and drink milk?

One day, the cat said, "Master, give me a pair of boots and a sack and you will see that I am not as useless as you think." It was a very strange request for a cat to make, but it was granted nonetheless.

The cat, or Puss in Boots, as the miller's son now called him, went into the forest and caught a rabbit. He put it in the sack and then instead of taking it home to the miller's son, he took it to the King's palace.

"Please accept this small present from my master the Marquis of Carabas," said Puss in Boots.

It was to be the first of many presents Puss in Boots took to the King, and each time he said he had been sent by his master the Marquis of Carabas. And although the King never actually met the Marquis of Carabas, he soon became very familiar with his name. The miller's son knew nothing of the presents, or of the Marquis of Carabas, and Puss in Boots didn't tell him.

One day, when Puss in Boots was at the palace, he overheard someone say that the King was about to take his daughter for a drive in the country. Puss in Boots hurried home.

"Quick master!" he called. "Go and bathe in the river and I will make your fortune."

It was another strange request for a cat to make but the miller's son was used to his pet by now and so he did as he was told. No sooner was he in the river than Puss in Boots took his clothes and threw them into the river with him.

"Puss . . . Puss . . . what are you doing?" called the miller's son.

Puss didn't answer, he was watching the road. Presently he saw the King's carriage in the distance. He waited until it was close then ran out in the road in front of it.

"Help! Help! My master the Marquis of Carabas is drowning! Please save him!"

75

It took but a moment to drag the miller's son, who hadn't the slightest idea what Puss in Boots was up to, from the river and find him some dry clothes. He looked so handsome in the fine velvet tunic and the doublet and hose borrowed from one of the footmen that the princess fell in love with him at once.

"Father dear, may the Marquis of Carabas ride with us?"

The King liked to please his daughter and agreed to her request at once.

"Will you ride with us Puss?" asked the King.

Puss asked to be excused. He said he had something rather important to attend to. He ran on ahead of the carriage, and each time he saw someone at work in the fields he called, "If the King asks who this land belongs to, tell him it belongs to the Marquis of Carabas."

The King did stop the carriage several times, and each time he received the same answer to his question.

'The Marquis of Carabas must be a very rich man,' he thought.

Puss in Boots ran so swiftly that soon he was a long way ahead of the carriage. Presently he came to a rich and imposing looking castle, which he knew belonged to a cruel and wicked ogre. He went straight up to the ogre without so much as a twitching of a whisker, and said, "I hear you can turn yourself into any animal you choose. I won't believe a story like that unless I see it for myself."

Immediately, the ogre changed himself into a lion, and roared and growled and snarled.

"There . . ." he said, when he had turned himself back into an ogre. "I hope I frightened you."

"It must be easy to change yourself into something big," said Puss in Boots with a shrug. "I don't suppose you can turn yourself into something as small as a . . . er . . . um . . ." He seemed to be thinking, ". . . er . . . um . . . a mouse?"

The ogre couldn't have a mere cat doubting his special abilities. He changed himself into a tiny mouse in the twinkling of an eye. It was the last time he changed himself into anything because Puss in Boots pounced on him and ate him up before he could change back into an ogre, and THAT was the end of him!

"Hoorah!" shouted the castle servants. "We are free of the wicked ogre at last. Hoorah!"

"Your new master will always be kind, you can be sure of that," said Puss in Boots.

"Who IS our new master?" they asked.

"The Marquis of Carabas of course," said Puss.

When the King's carriage reached the castle, Puss in Boots was standing at the drawbridge, with the smiling servants gathered round him.

"Welcome . . ." he said with a beautiful bow. "Welcome to the home of my master the Marquis of Carabas."

The miller's son was too astonished to do anything except think to himself, 'Whatever is Puss up to?'

Luckily Puss had time to explain while the King was getting out of the carriage.

'What a rich man this Marquis must be,' thought the King. 'And such a nice young man too.'

Not long afterwards the princess and the miller's son were married. They, and Puss in Boots, lived happily ever after in the castle that had once belonged to the wicked ogre.

THE BOASTING TRAVELLER

A traveller was boasting about the wonderful places he had been to and the clever things he had done. The people listening to him had grown bored of his constant showing off.

"Why," said the traveller loudly, "once, when I was in Rhodes, I entered a jumping competition. As a matter of fact, I jumped twice as far as anyone has ever jumped before. If you don't believe me, go to Rhodes and ask someone there."

"If you can really jump that far," said one of his audience, who had not believed one word the traveller had said, ". . . there is no need to go to Rhodes to prove it. You could do something else."

"What do you mean?" asked the puzzled traveller.

"Why," said the man, "you can jump here and prove it to us now."

Moral: *Deeds speak louder than words.*

JUPITER AND THE MONKEY

There was great excitement among the animals. The god Jupiter was going to give a prize to the animal who had the most beautiful baby.

From all over the jungle they gathered. They came from the hills and the valleys, the plains and the rivers. They all brought their babies with them to be judged.

With a great fanfare of trumpets, the god Jupiter arrived among them, coming down from the skies. He walked among the hundreds of animals, looking at each baby very carefully before making up his mind.

One of the animals was a monkey, clutching her child. Jupiter stopped and laughed when he saw the flat-nosed, hairless little baby.

"What on earth are you doing here?" he roared. "You have no chance of winning the prize. I have never seen such an odd-looking little creature in my life!"

The great god passed on. The monkey held her child close to her.

"I don't care what Jupiter or anyone else thinks," she whispered. "To me you are the most beautiful baby in the world."

Moral: *Beauty is in the eye of the beholder.*

THE GRASSHOPPER AND THE ANTS

All through the long summer days, the ants had worked away gathering food to store for the winter days when snow lay deep on the ground.

As they gathered their food and put it in their store-house the idle grasshopper looked at them and laughed.

"Poor fools!" he called. "Why do you work when the sun is high in the sky? This is a time for singing and playing."

The ants paid no attention to him. They went on working hard, collecting enough food to see them through the long winter days and nights. As they did so the grasshopper lay in the sun, singing happily.

But in the end the summer went away. Winter ruled in the land, covering everything with snow and ice. There was no food to be seen anywhere. The grasshopper, who had stored no food in the summer months, was starving. He limped along to the store-house where the ants had stored their food.

"What do you want?" asked the ants, as they carried on sweeping, tidying and sorting. The ants were always busy.

"I am very hungry," begged the grasshopper. "Please give me some of the food you have saved, or I will starve to death."

"You should have thought of that in the summer when you were busy with your playing and singing," said the ants. "If you spent the summer singing, then maybe you should spend the winter dancing, and not bother about eating at all."

The ants would not give the grasshopper a single scrap of their food, and he went away sad and hungry.

Moral: *We should always make plans for the future.*

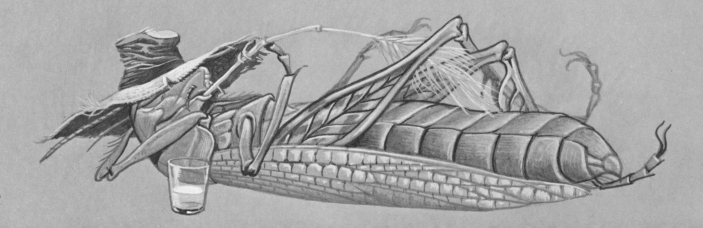

THE DONKEY AND HIS SHADOW

A traveller hired a donkey to take him to the next town. He agreed a fee with the owner of the donkey.

"There is just one drawback," explained the donkey's owner. "My beast won't walk very far unless I hit him with a stick now and again. You ride on his back, and I'll walk along behind you both with a stick, until we reach the town."

It was a very hot day, but the two men made good progress, the traveller riding on the donkey and the owner walking behind with a stick to prod the donkey. In the middle of the day, with the sun at its hottest, they stopped for a rest.

"I shall sit in the shade of the donkey," said the traveller, dismounting.

"Oh no you won't," snapped the donkey's owner. "That's where I'm going to rest. It's the only shade for miles around."

"I've hired the donkey, so I should sit in its shade," argued the traveller.

"Not at all," shouted the owner. "You only hired the donkey, you did not hire its shadow. That belongs to me."

The owner was so angry that he gave the traveller a push. The traveller pushed back. The owner hit the traveller. The traveller hit the owner back. In a moment, the two men were standing toe to toe, fighting furiously.

While the two men fought over his shadow, the donkey grew bored and trotted off over the hill. Soon he was out of sight, taking his shadow with him.

Moral: *Most arguments are useless.*

THE TWO POTS

The river was in flood, sweeping everything along with it. On top of the water, bobbing helplessly along, were two pots. One of the pots was made from the strong mixture of metals known as brass. The other pot was just as beautiful but it was not nearly as strong, because it was made out of clay.

"Come over here and stay close to me," the brass pot invited the clay pot. "I will look after you. I am very strong. Nothing can break me. I might dent a little, but that is all. As for you, poor thing, I know how weak clay pots are. You are so easily broken. Come here, I say, and let me guard you."

"No, thank you," called out the clay pot, keeping as far away from the brass pot as it possibly could.

"Why not?" asked the brass pot, rather hurt. "Why won't you float down the river with me?"

"Well, I know you mean your offer kindly," said the clay pot, drifting away quickly, "but you are so much stronger than I am. One tiny knock from you and I would break into a thousand pieces."

Moral: *Equals make the best friends.*

THE WILD BOAR AND THE FOX

A fox was trotting through the forest. He noticed how peaceful everything seemed. He could hear no sounds of wild animals fighting each other, and there were no signs of any hunters in search of prey.

"How nice this is," thought the fox as he went on his way.

After a time he came across a wild boar. This animal was busily sharpening its tusks on a tree, rubbing them against the bark. The fox stopped to watch.

"You silly animal," he yawned. "Why are you wasting your time doing that? There is no need for it. It is a very quiet day here in the forest. There are no hunters about to fear."

"You may be right," grunted the boar, not stopping, "but that isn't the point. When my life is in danger, I must be ready to defend myself at once. I won't have time to stop and sharpen my tusks first!"

Moral: *Be prepared.*

THE WOLF AND THE HORSE

A wolf was slinking across the fields, looking for some mischief he could do. He passed by a field of oats, waving in the soft breeze. The wolf stopped hopefully, sniffing around for the scent of some small creature he could hunt down and eat. There was no sign of any living thing, however, so the crest-fallen animal went on his way across the fields.

Some time later, the wolf met a horse. The hair on the wolf's back rose and he snarled to himself. But he said nothing to annoy the horse. The wolf hated all other creatures, but he was not going to fall out with one as big and as strong as the horse.

Instead the crafty wolf cast about in his mind for some way of making himself agreeable to the horse. Out of the corner of his eye he saw the field of oats waving in the wind.

"Look at that fine field of oats over there," he said. "I saw you coming and I know horses like eating oats, so I left them all for you. Wasn't that kind of me?"

"You don't fool me," grunted the horse, not at all impressed. "I know that wolves don't eat oats. If you did they would all be gone by now."

Moral: *There is no virtue in giving someone something we do not want ourselves.*

THE MICE IN COUNCIL

A cat was chasing all the mice and killing those she caught. The mice called a great meeting to try to think of some way of making themselves safe from the cat.

The meeting lasted a long time. Many ideas were put forward by the mice at the council, but none of them seemed any good. Finally one bright young mouse stepped forward.

"I've got it!" he said excitedly. "The reason why the cat catches so many of us is that we don't hear her coming. Is that right?"

"Of course it is," said another mouse. "That doesn't help us much."

"I haven't finished yet," the first mouse told him impatiently. "What we need is something to warn us of the cat's approach. Well, I know what to do. We must tie a bell round the cat's neck. That way, every time the cat comes near us, we will hear the bell tinkling and have time to hide."

"What a good idea!" squeaked the other mice. "Well done! You have solved all our problems. All we have to do is find a bell and tie it round that old cat's neck."

The other mice started to cheer and squeal excitedly, but then an old and very wise mouse who had taken no part in the meeting so far spoke up from a corner.

"Just a minute," he said. "It may be a good idea, but tell me this. Is anyone here willing to risk his life by going up to the cat and putting the bell round his neck?"

No one answered. In a moment all the mice had left the meeting and the room was empty. No one was prepared to put the bell on the cat.

Moral: *It is no use having bright ideas unless we are willing to put them into practice.*

THE BRAVE LITTLE TAILOR

One day, a tailor was sitting at his bench sewing a seam with his needle and thread. Beside him was a plate and on the plate was a slice of bread and jam. It was his lunch and the sooner he finished sewing the seam the sooner he could eat it. He liked jam spread on bread. He wasn't the only one.

"Jam . . ." buzzed the greedy flies. "We smell jam."

"Don't you dare!" shouted the little tailor. He picked up a piece of cloth. "Take that!" he shouted, and he swatted at the flies as hard as he could. Seven of them fell dead on the table.

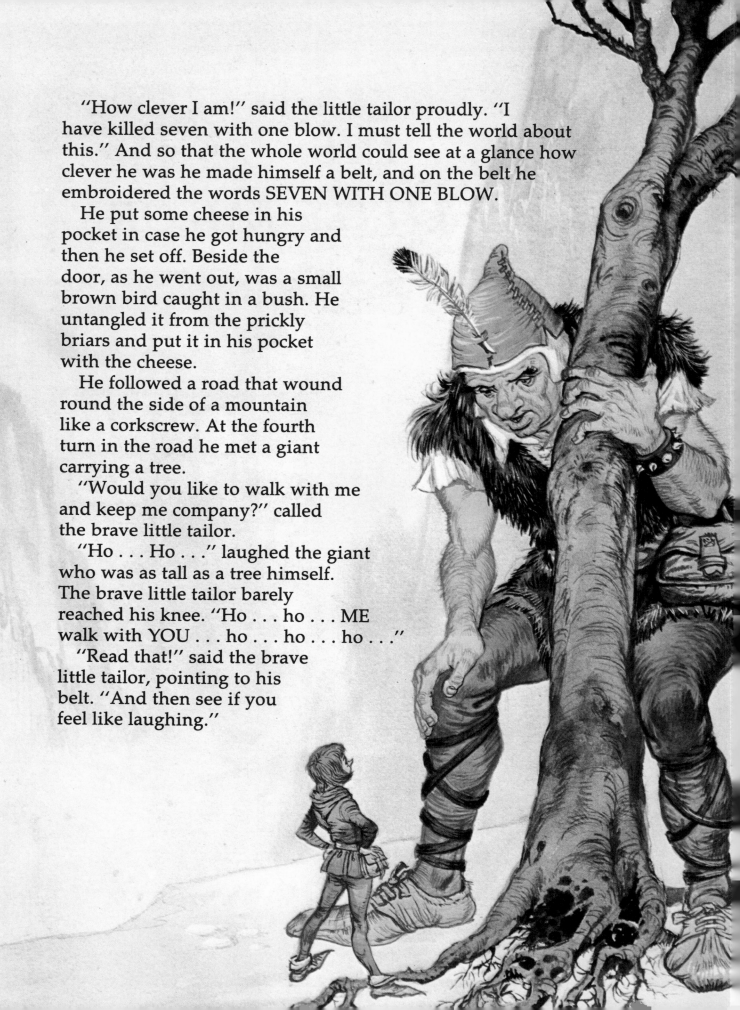

"How clever I am!" said the little tailor proudly. "I have killed seven with one blow. I must tell the world about this." And so that the whole world could see at a glance how clever he was he made himself a belt, and on the belt he embroidered the words SEVEN WITH ONE BLOW.

He put some cheese in his pocket in case he got hungry and then he set off. Beside the door, as he went out, was a small brown bird caught in a bush. He untangled it from the prickly briars and put it in his pocket with the cheese.

He followed a road that wound round the side of a mountain like a corkscrew. At the fourth turn in the road he met a giant carrying a tree.

"Would you like to walk with me and keep me company?" called the brave little tailor.

"Ho . . . Ho . . ." laughed the giant who was as tall as a tree himself. The brave little tailor barely reached his knee. "Ho . . . ho . . . ME walk with YOU . . . ho . . . ho . . . ho . . ."

"Read that!" said the brave little tailor, pointing to his belt. "And then see if you feel like laughing."

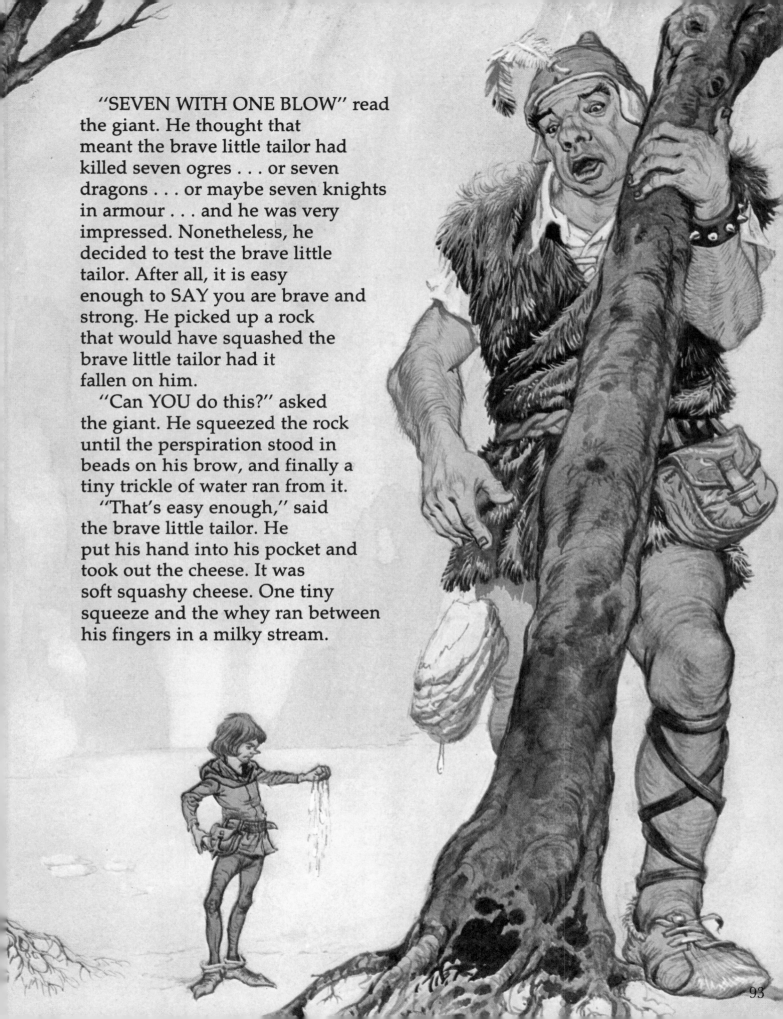

"SEVEN WITH ONE BLOW" read the giant. He thought that meant the brave little tailor had killed seven ogres . . . or seven dragons . . . or maybe seven knights in armour . . . and he was very impressed. Nonetheless, he decided to test the brave little tailor. After all, it is easy enough to SAY you are brave and strong. He picked up a rock that would have squashed the brave little tailor had it fallen on him.

"Can YOU do this?" asked the giant. He squeezed the rock until the perspiration stood in beads on his brow, and finally a tiny trickle of water ran from it.

"That's easy enough," said the brave little tailor. He put his hand into his pocket and took out the cheese. It was soft squashy cheese. One tiny squeeze and the whey ran between his fingers in a milky stream.

"Oh!" said the giant, rather taken aback. Then he said, "Can YOU throw as far as this?" He picked up a small boulder and hurled it with all his might. It flew through the air like a thunderbolt and landed with a thud on the grass, at least half a league away.

"Easily," said the brave little tailor. This time he took the little brown bird from his pocket. It had got over its fright at being tangled in the briar and was glad to be free. When the brave little tailor tossed it into the air, it flew and flew until it was just a tiny speck in the distance.

"It will fall to the ground sooner or later," said the brave little tailor. "Probably later rather then sooner."

"If you're THAT strong," said the giant, feeling more than a little put out, "you can help me carry this tree home."

"Glad to," said the brave little tailor. "You go in front and take the roots, I'll follow behind and carry the branches, which are the heaviest part."

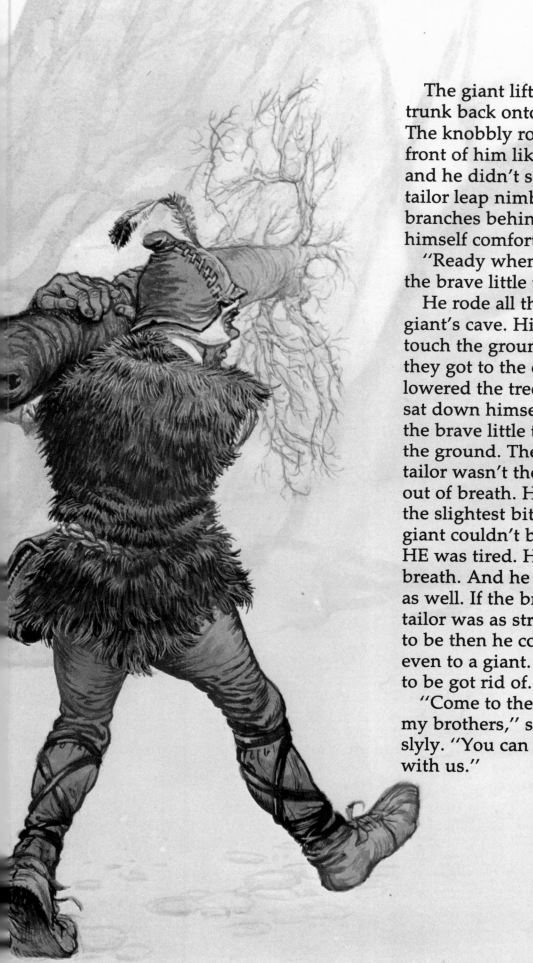

The giant lifted the heavy trunk back onto his shoulder. The knobbly roots stuck out in front of him like a lopsided beard and he didn't see the brave little tailor leap nimbly into the branches behind him and settle himself comfortably.

"Ready when you are!" called the brave little tailor.

He rode all the way to the giant's cave. His feet didn't touch the ground once. When they got to the cave the giant lowered the tree to the ground and sat down himself. He didn't see the brave little tailor jump to the ground. The brave little tailor wasn't the slightest bit out of breath. He didn't look the slightest bit tired. The giant couldn't believe his eyes. HE was tired. HE was out of breath. And he was frightened as well. If the brave little tailor was as strong as he seemed to be then he could be dangerous, even to a giant. He would have to be got rid of.

"Come to the cave and meet my brothers," said the giant slyly. "You can spend the night with us."

That night, the giant let the brave little tailor sleep in his own bed, while he slept on the floor. The bed was just the right size, and comfortable for a giant, but for the brave little tailor it was too big and far too uncomfortable. Each lump in the mattress felt like a small mountain. He could not sleep at all and at last he crawled into a corner and fell asleep there. And what a good thing he did, for in the night, the giant smote the bed with an iron bar. If the brave little tailor had been sleeping in it he would surely have been killed.

The next morning the giants were having breakfast, happy in the thought that the brave little tailor who had killed seven with one blow, was now dead himself. They had the surprise of their lives when the brave little tailor called for his breakfast.

They bellowed with fright and
ran from the cave. They ran
until they came to the sea and
they splashed through that until
they reached the land on the far
side. They are probably running
still. The brave little tailor
puffed out his chest when he
saw the three giants running away
from HIM. He felt brave enough
to conquer a hundred giants.

He tricked a lot of people
into believing he was stronger
than he really was. Even kings
trembled at the thought of what
he might do. One day he became
a king himself, but that is a
story for another time.

THE BIRDS, BEASTS AND BAT

The birds and beasts were at war. Their battles were fierce and frequent. Sometimes the birds won, swooping down out of the sun and attacking the animals. Sometimes the beasts won, creeping up on the birds as they searched for food on the ground, and leaping on them.

But there was one creature who was always on the winning side. He never lost, because he kept on changing sides. He would fight for the birds until they looked like losing, and then change sides. For a time he would fight for the animals, and then if the birds gained the upper hand, he would change back and join *them*.

This creature was the bat. He thought he was a very clever fellow, always being on the winning side.

In the end the war ended. The birds and the beasts agreed to live in peace for ever.

"Now I shall get my reward," the bat told himself. "Everyone will think I'm a fine fellow. After all, *I* was never on the losing side. I helped both sides. In fact, the birds and the beasts may make me their king!"

It did not work out like that at all. Neither the birds nor the beasts would have anything to do with him!

"You are a traitor!" they told the amazed bat. "You are loyal to no one. You only serve yourself. You let down both sides in the war. We want nothing more to do with you."

From that day to this the bat was an outcast, ignored by both the birds and the beasts.

Moral: *People are expected to be loyal and to stick by their friends.*

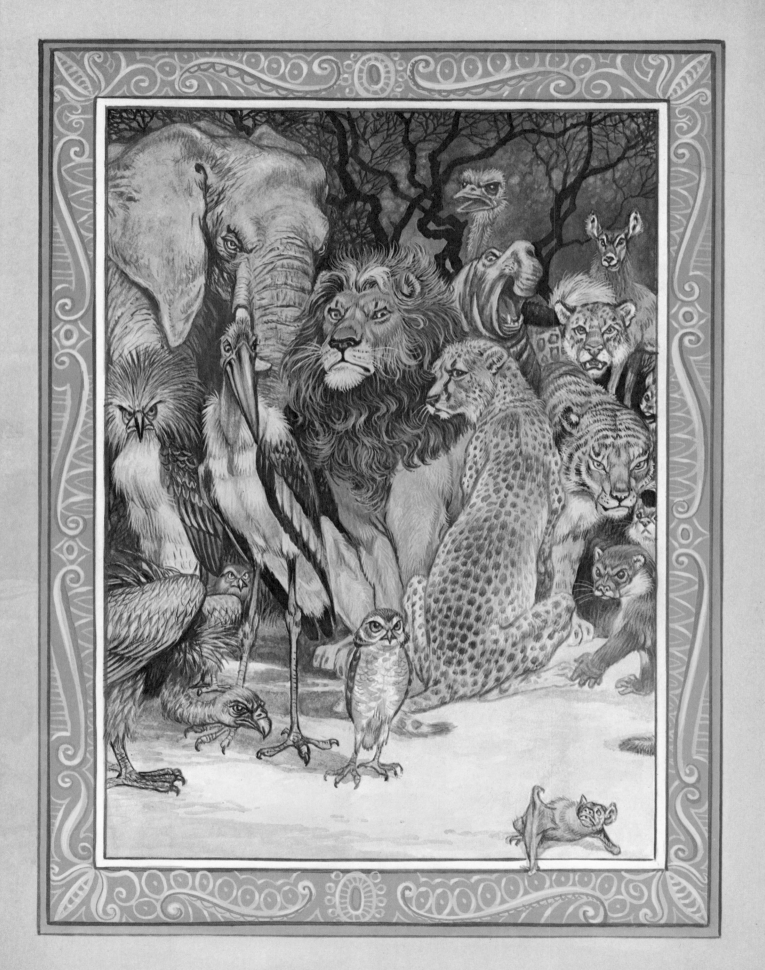

HERCULES AND THE WAGONER

A man was driving his horse and wagon along a muddy lane when the wheels of his cart sank deep into the mud. The man got down and tried to push the wagon along. It was no use. The wagon was stuck.

The man lifted his head and cried in despair. "Everything happens to me!" he wailed. "Why doesn't someone come and help me? What about the mighty Hercules? He is the strongest man on earth. Where is he now that I need him?"

Hercules heard his name being called and came to see what was wanted of him.

"Stop moaning and put your own shoulder to the wheel," he told the wagoner sternly. "How can you expect others to help you, if you do not help yourself? If you show that you are willing to do your share, I will gladly help you."

Moral: *Heaven helps those who help themselves.*

THE OX AND THE FROGS

A family of frogs lived happily in the rushes of a pool. The two little frogs in the family spent hours every day playing happily at the side of this pool. They made friends with all the other occupants of the pool and all the animals who came to drink the water there.

One day, however, a dreadful accident took place. A great ox came lumbering down to the water's edge to drink. This beast was so big that he did not notice the two little frogs. As he made his way to the edge of the pool, he trod on one of them and squashed him flat.

Sadly the remaining little frog went home and reported to his mother what had happened at the water's edge.

"A great big creature trod on my brother and killed him," he wailed.

"How big was this animal?" demanded his mother. She puffed out her cheeks and her sides. "Was he as big as this?" she asked.

"Oh, much, much bigger than that," replied the little frog.

The frog's mother puffed and puffed and puffed. She made herself as big and as round as a very fat pumpkin.

"Was he as big as . . . ." she began – but then she burst.

Moral: *There are some things which it is better not to know.*

102

THE GNAT AND THE BULL

The gnat was a small insect but it had a great idea of its own importance. One fine day it grew tired of flying and landed on the horn of a great bull grazing in a field. The animal went on chewing, taking no notice of the small gnat. The insect rested in the sun until it felt ready to carry on flying. Before it left it looked down politely at the bull.

"I'm afraid I must be on my way now," it said. "Thank you for allowing me to rest on your horn. I would like to stay and chat, but I should be on my way."

"I couldn't care less what you do," grunted the bull. "I did not notice you come, and I shall not notice when you go."

Moral: *We often seem more important to ourselves than we do to others.*

THUMBLING

There are many stories about Thumbling, the boy who was no bigger than a thumb. All adventures have to begin somewhere, and this story tells how one of Thumbling's began.

Thumbling's father was going into the forest to cut wood.

"I do wish someone could bring the cart to me when I have finished," he sighed, "then I wouldn't have to come all the way home to fetch it."

"I'll bring it to you," said Thumbling.

"How can you?" laughed Thumbling's father. "You are far too small to lead the horse."

"That may be so," said Thumbling, "but if Mother harnesses the horse for me I will sit in his ear, and tell him where to go."

It seemed a good idea, so Thumbling's father went off with his axe over his shoulder. "Make sure you're not late," he said.

"I won't be," said Thumbling.

When it was time, Thumbling's mother harnessed the horse, Thumbling climbed into the horse's ear, and off they went.

"Gee up!" cried Thumbling, who for such a small boy had an astonishingly loud voice. "Gee up!" The horse wasn't too keen on being shouted at from inside his own ear and set off at a brisk trot. "To the right!" shouted Thumbling, when he wanted the horse to go to the right. "To the left!" shouted Thumbling when he wanted him to go to the left. "Straight on!" he shouted when he wanted him to go neither to the left, nor to the right. They were almost at the place where they were to meet Thumbling's father, when they passed two men.

"That's very strange," said one of the men. "I can hear the driver of that horse and cart, but I can't see him."

"Let's follow it, and see where it goes," said his companion.

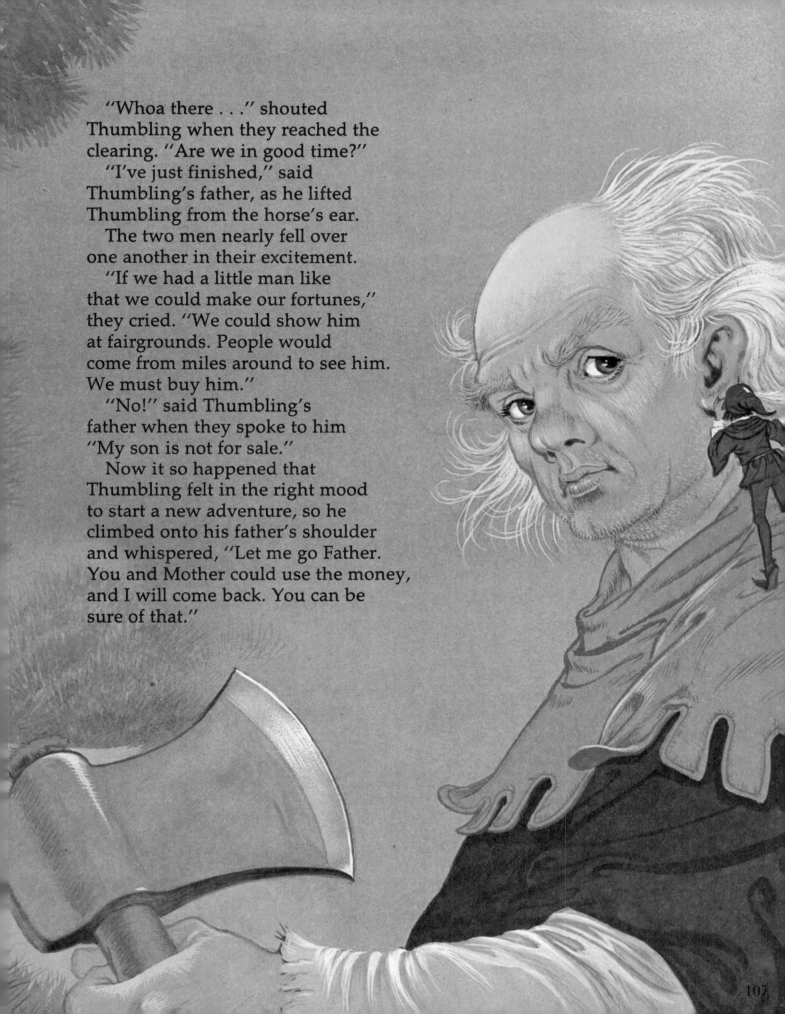

"Whoa there . . ." shouted Thumbling when they reached the clearing. "Are we in good time?"

"I've just finished," said Thumbling's father, as he lifted Thumbling from the horse's ear.

The two men nearly fell over one another in their excitement.

"If we had a little man like that we could make our fortunes," they cried. "We could show him at fairgrounds. People would come from miles around to see him. We must buy him."

"No!" said Thumbling's father when they spoke to him "My son is not for sale."

Now it so happened that Thumbling felt in the right mood to start a new adventure, so he climbed onto his father's shoulder and whispered, "Let me go Father. You and Mother could use the money, and I will come back. You can be sure of that."

So, Thumbling's father, who was used to his son's ways, said the two men could take him in exchange for a bag of gold, if they first helped him load the logs onto the cart.

"Where will you sit?" asked one of the men, when Thumbling had waved goodbye to his father.

"On the brim of your hat," said Thumbling.

"Is he still there?" asked the man who was wearing the hat, every few minutes. Because he was wearing the hat he couldn't see what was happening on the brim.

"We mustn't lose him."

Sometimes, when they checked Thumbling was at the front of the hat. Sometimes he was at the back. Sometimes he was looking where they were going. Sometimes he was looking where they had been. Sometimes he was lying on his back, looking up at the endless blue sky.

The two men walked a long way. Just as it was beginning to get dark, they sat down on a grassy bank to rest.

"Take your hat off," said Thumbling.

"Why should I do that?" asked the man wearing the hat.

"Because it's bad manners to keep your hat on ALL the time," said Thumbling. "And anyway, if you don't take your hat off sometimes your head will get too hot and your hair will fall out."

"You could be right," said the man, and took off his hat and laid it on the grass.

Quick as a grasshopper, Thumbling jumped off the brim, and ran through the grass until he came to a mousehole. Down he went.

The two men were furious.

"Come out!" they shouted. "We have been tricked!" they shouted even louder. It didn't matter how much they shouted, or how hard they poked their sticks down the mousehole, Thumbling would NOT come out. Eventually it became too dark to see where the hole was any more and they had to go home without him.

Now Thumbling was free to go where he wanted and do what he liked. He slept in the mousehole that night and next day he went to look for adventure. It was a long time before he got home again, but he did get there in the end. He always did at the end of ALL his adventures.

THE FOX AND THE STORK

A fox decided to play a joke upon a stork. In order to do this he invited the bird to dinner in his den. When the stork arrived, the fox served a delicious soup in a flat dish.

"Mm, this soup tastes good," said the fox, lapping it greedily from the dish, his nose only a few inches from it. "What do you think of it, my friend?"

"How can I tell?" asked the stork bitterly, pecking vainly at the flat dish with her long beak. "This dish is too flat. I cannot get any soup into my mouth at all."

This was just what the sly old fox had hoped would happen. He had upset the stork and made her look silly. He thought this very funny and finished the soup himself with a sly smile upon his face. The stork made one or two more efforts to peck at the soup, but then gave up and went home, deciding to get her own back on the fox.

A few days later the stork had made her plans. She invited the fox to come and have dinner with her in her home by the water's edge. She

too, prepared soup for the meal. She served it in a jug which was wide at the bottom and narrow at the top.

"Let us begin," said the stork, dipping her head into the jug and taking a long sip. "Mm, this is good! What do you think of it, my friend?"

"How can I tell?" grumbled the fox, trying in vain to get his head into the mouth of the jug. "I cannot reach the soup to lap it up!"

"What a shame," said the stork calmly.

She said nothing else, but finished the soup herself, while the fox looked on in a bad temper.

In the end, the fox went home in a bad mood. The tables had been turned on him, but for some reason he did not think it was funny.

Moral: *Something which seems funny when it happens to someone else may not seem so funny when it happens to us.*

111

THE LION AND THE MOUSE

The lion was proud and strong, and king of the jungle. One day while he was sleeping, a tiny mouse ran over his face. The great lion awoke with a snarl. He caught the mouse with one mighty paw and raised the other to squash the tiny creature who had annoyed him.

"Oh, please, mighty lion!" squeaked the mouse, "please do not kill me. Let me go, I beg you. If you do, one day I may be able to help you in some way."

This greatly amused the lion. The thought that such a small and frightened creature as a mouse might be able to help the king of the jungle was so funny that he did not have the heart to kill the mouse.

"Go away," he growled.

A few days later, a party of hunters came into the jungle. They decided to try to capture the lion. They climbed two trees, one on either side of the path, and held a net over the path.

Later in the day the lion came loping along the path. At once the hunters dropped their net on the great beast. The lion roared and fought mightily, but he could not escape from the net.

The hunters went off to eat, leaving the lion trapped in the net, unable to move. The lion roared for help, but the only creature in the jungle who dared come near was the tiny mouse.

"Oh, it's you," groaned the lion. "There's nothing you can do to help me. You're too small."

"I may be small," said the mouse, "but I have sharp teeth and I owe you a good turn!"

Then the mouse began to nibble at the net. Before long he had made a hole big enough to allow the lion to crawl through and make his escape into the jungle.

Moral: *Sometimes the weak are able to help the strong.*

JUPITER AND THE TORTOISE

Thousands of years ago, the tortoise did not carry his shell with him. Then something happened which saw to it that for ever more the tortoise and his shell were always together.

It started when the great god, Jupiter, invited all the animals to a great feast. Every animal that lived came to this feast, except for the tortoise.

Jupiter was so disappointed. He had hoped that every creature under the sun would come to his feast, but the tortoise had spoiled that.

"Perhaps he is ill," worried the god. "I had better go and see."

So Jupiter made his way to the home of the tortoise. When he arrived he found the creature looking perfectly well.

"Why didn't you come to my feast?" asked the god.

"I didn't feel like it," yawned the tortoise. "I wanted to stay at home instead."

"Indeed?" said the god angrily. "In that case for the rest of time, wherever you go, you had better carry your home with you."

And that is just what happened, from that day to this.

Moral: *We had better be careful what we say in case people take us at our word.*

114

THE SHEPHERDESS
AND THE SWEEP

Once there was a shepherdess. Not a real shepherdess but
a delicate porcelain one. She was very beautiful. She stood
beside the porcelain sweep, on a table, in a dark and crowded
parlour. The sweep was as black as coal, except for his face and hands
which were as pink and as clean as the shepherdess's own. Just
behind them stood the Chinese mandarin. He had a black stubby
pig-tail hanging down his back, and grey slanting eyes. The
Chinese mandarin nodded all the time. He couldn't help it.
It was the way he was made. The shepherdess called him Grandpa,
though he wasn't, because if he had been she would have
been Chinese too, and she wasn't.

On the far side of the room and facing the table where the
three porcelain figures stood, was a carved wooden cabinet. Carved
in the very middle of the door was a very peculiar man. He had
a lop-sided smile that was hardly a smile at all, and a beard, and
legs like a goat. The children who lived in the house and sometimes
came into the parlour called him Mr. Goat-legged, Commanding
General, Private, Sergeant, because they thought it suited him,
though if they were in a hurry they called him Mr. Goat-legs.

115

One day, Mr. Goat-legs asked the Chinese
mandarin if he could marry the shepherdess.
The Chinese mandarin nodded, as was his habit.

"Good," said Mr. Goat-legs looking pleased.

"But Grandpa, I don't want to marry horrid
Mr. Goat-legs," said the shepherdess.

"It is too late now. I have given my
consent," said the Chinese mandarin. "The
wedding will be tonight. Wake me up in time
for the ceremony." And with no more ado, he
nodded himself to sleep.

The little shepherdess cried tears that
looked like seed pearls. The sweep tried to
comfort her.

"Please take me away from the parlour and
out into the wide world," she pleaded. "I
cannot marry Mr. Goat-legs."

The running stags carved on the side of
the cabinet saw them climbing down to the floor.

"The shepherdess and the sweep are
running away!" they cried.

The mandarin woke with a start and began
nodding so furiously, his whole body rocked
backwards and forwards. The shepherdess and
the sweep had never seen him so angry and
were very frightened.

"There is only one way to escape," whispered the sweep. "We must go into the stove and up the chimney to the roof."

It was a difficult climb, even for the sweep. It was dark, and sooty, and steep. The shepherdess was afraid she would slip. If she fell she knew she would break into a thousand pieces.

"Do not look down," whispered the sweep as he followed behind and guided her feet to the nooks and crannies. "Look up towards the star which shines at the end of our journey."

When the shepherdess looked up through the dark tunnel of the chimney, she could see a tiny speck of light, far, far away in the distance. The higher they climbed the bigger it grew, and when they got to the top it became the entire sky.

The shepherdess and the sweep sat side by side on the rim of the chimney-pot and looked wearily across the rooftops at the wide, wide world. The shepherdess did not like what she saw. The big wide world was so very big, and so very wide. She began to cry again.

"Please take me back to the parlour," she sobbed. "I like the big wide world even less than I like Mr. Goat-legs." Her face was stained with sooty tears. The little sweep could not bear to see her so unhappy and agreed to take her back.

The journey down the chimney was just as difficult as the journey up had been. It was just as dark. Just as frightening. When they finally crawled out of the stove and into the parlour they were met by a strange and eerie silence.

"Something has happened!" cried the shepherdess. "Oh I just know something dreadful has happened!"

It had. In his anger, the Chinese mandarin had rolled off the edge of the table and now he was lying in pieces on the floor.

"Oh dear, it's all our fault," cried the shepherdess. "Oh poor Grandpa . . . what are we to do?" And she cried even more.

"We can't do anything," said the sweep, "but don't worry. Someone is sure to come along and glue him together again."

And someone did. But from that day onwards he lost his habit of nodding. It didn't matter how many times Mr. Goat-legs asked if he could still marry the shepherdess, the Chinese mandarin, would not, could not, nod and give his consent. And so the shepherdess and the sweep were able to stand side by side until the end of their days.

THE ASTRONOMER

An absent-minded astronomer was interested in nothing but the stars. Every night he would go out and study them in the sky.

One evening he was walking along as usual, his head in the air and his eyes fixed on the stars. He did not notice that there was a deep well in front of him. As he made his way along, he suddenly tripped and fell into the well.

"Help!" he shouted. "Help me someone!"

He sat at the bottom of the well, soaked to the skin and calling for help. A passer-by heard his shouts and peered down the hole at him.

"Please help me," begged the astronomer. "I was so busy looking at the stars, I did not notice this hole."

"That's your fault," the passer-by told him. "You should have looked where you were going."

Moral: *It is no use fixing our minds on higher things if we ignore what is going on around us.*

THE FISHERMAN AND THE SPRAT

It had been a bad day for the poor fisherman. He had sailed his small craft out into the wide sea at dawn. All day he had been casting his nets into the water and then drawing them out again. Each time he did so, the nets remained empty.

"Can there be a single fish left in the sea, I wonder?" the man grumbled. "It certainly doesn't seem so."

He was about to give up and sail sadly back to port, when he drew in his nets for the last time. Something was wriggling in the bottom of one of the nets. His heart leaping, the fisherman hurried forward to see what he had caught. To his disgust he saw that he had caught one small sprat, the tiniest of fish.

This particular sprat was so small that it fitted easily into the palm of the fisherman's hand.

"Please let me go," begged the small fish. "You can see for yourself that I am no use to you as I am. But if you throw me back into the water, I shall grow up into a fine big fish. Then you can catch me again in a year's time, when I will make a meal."

"No way," said the man. "If I let you go you would vanish!"

Moral: *A fish in the hand is worth two in the sea.*

THE LARK AND THE FARMER

When it was time to build her nest the lark did so in a field of corn, not in a tree like most other birds. She laid her eggs in this nest and watched them hatch out into young birds. Life was very good among the waving corn.

Then one day, the farmer who owned the field came walking across to look at it.

"Hmm, very nice," he said. "This corn is just about ready to harvest. I think I'll have a word with my neighbours and ask them to help me gather it in."

At this the young larks were very frightened and set up a great twittering.

"Quick, mother, we must move before our nest is destroyed!"

Their mother was too wise to be worried by such talk.

"Hush, my darlings," she soothed. "There is nothing to worry about yet. A man who talks about going to his neighbours for help can be in no great hurry. We can wait a little longer."

A few days later, when the corn was so ripe it was falling to the ground, the farmer walked across the field again.

"I must hire some men and gather in this corn at once," he said.

"Come, my children," sighed the mother lark. "Now the farmer is relying upon himself, not others. It is time for us to move."

Moral: *If we really want something done, it is best to do it ourselves.*

THE FOX AND THE BRAMBLE

The fox was tired and hungry. He had been prowling over the fields all day, looking for food. Now he was on his way home and he was in no mood to be delayed.

He came to a hedge which stood between him and his lair. He ought to walk along the side of the hedge until he found a hole, but he was too tired and fed-up to bother. He decided to push his way through the hedge, and so save time.

The fox leapt across the ditch towards the hedge. As he did so, his foot slipped. Desperately the fox thrust out his paws and caught hold of a bramble to stop himself falling. The bramble scratched the fox badly.

"I would have been better off letting myself fall, than ask you for help," he complained sourly.

"You should have had more sense than to clutch a bramble," said the hedge.

Moral: *We should use our judgement before coming to a decision.*

THE UGLY DUCKLING

Once, somewhere in the country, there was a duck who had a clutch of eggs to hatch. Five of them hatched into fluffy little ducklings, but the sixth, which for some reason was bigger than all the others, lay in the nest, smooth and unbroken.

"That's much too big to be a duck egg," said one of the duck's friends. "Looks more like a turkey egg to me."

"How will I be able to tell?" asked the duck.

"It will not swim when it is hatched," said her friend. "Turkeys never do."

But the egg wasn't a turkey egg because the bird that hatched from it DID swim. It swam as well as any duckling.

"That last duckling of yours is very ugly," laughed the farmyard hens. It was true. He wasn't a bit like his brothers and sisters.

"What an ugly duckling," laughed the geese when they saw him. And somehow that name stuck. Whenever anyone wanted him they called, "Ugly duckling, where are you?" or if they didn't want him they said, "Ugly duckling, go away." He even thought of himself as an ugly duckling. He was very sad. He didn't like being ugly. He didn't like being teased. No one would play with him. No one would swim with him. Even his mother made fun of him. One day, the ugly duckling ran away. And I am sorry to say, no one missed him at all.

The ugly duckling hoped he would find someone in the big wide world, to be his friend. Someone who wouldn't mind how ugly he was. But the wild ducks were just as unkind as the farmyard ducks, and the wild geese honked at him and made fun, just as the farmyard geese had done.

"Am I never to find a friend? Am I never to be happy?" sighed the ugly duckling.

One day, as he sat alone and unhappy in the middle of a lake on the bleak flat marshes, he heard the steady beat of wings. When he looked up there were swans flying overhead with their long necks stretched before them and their white feathers gleaming in the sun. They were so beautiful. If only he had been born a swan. But he hadn't. He had been born a duckling and an ugly one at that.

The ugly duckling stayed on the lake all through the long hard winter. Food was hard to find and he was often hungry. Once he was trapped in some ice and thought he would die. He was set free, just in time, by a farmer and his dog.

Spring came and the lake where he had spent the lonely winter became a busy, exciting, and noisy place. The ducks were forever quacking and the geese were forever honking. There was plenty of splashing and excitement. But not for the ugly duckling. No one quacked the latest piece of gossip to him. Sadly he spread his wings and took to the sky. He had never flown before and he was surprised how strong his wings were. They carried him away from the lake and the marshes and over a leafy garden.

On a still, clear pond in the garden, he could see the beautiful white swans, with their gracefully arched necks, and suddenly the ugly duckling felt that he did not want to live any longer.

"I will go down to the pond and ask those beautiful birds to kill me," he said. And down he went to the water. He bent his head humbly and closed his eyes.

"Kill me," he said to the swans. "I am too ugly to live."

"Ugly?" said the swans. "Have you looked at your reflection?"

"I do not need to look. I know how ugly I am," said the ugly duckling.

"Look into the water," said the swans. And so the ugly duckling did. What he saw made his heart beat fast and filled him with happiness. During the long winter months he had changed.

"I'm . . . I'm just like you . . ." he whispered.

When the children who lived in the garden came to feed the swans they called to one another, "A new swan . . . a new swan . . . isn't he beautiful?" And then the ugly duckling knew without a doubt that he really WAS a swan, that he had ALWAYS been a swan and that his days of being lonely were over.

THE DOG AND HIS REFLECTION

A dog was feeling very proud of himself. He had found a large piece of meat and was carrying it away in his mouth, so that he could eat it in peace somewhere.

He came to a stream and began to cross over a narrow plank which led from one bank to the other. Suddenly he stopped and looked down. In the surface of the water he saw his own reflection shining up at him.

The dog did not realise what it was. He thought that he was looking at another dog with a piece of meat in its mouth.

"Hello, that piece of meat is bigger than mine," he thought. "I'll grab it and run."

At that he dropped his own piece of meat in order to snatch the piece the other dog had. Of course his piece of meat fell into the stream and sank to the bottom, leaving the dog with nothing.

Moral: *Be content with what you have.*

THE SPENDTHRIFT AND THE SWALLOW

A man came into a fortune. Instead of putting some by in a safe place for his old age, he set out to spend all his money as quickly as he could. He became a spendthrift, someone who must buy everything he sees.

Before long, the foolish man had nothing left but the clothes he stood up in. He did not have a single coin left of all his fortune. Still he was not worried. He believed that the future would take care of itself. Somehow or other he would be all right.

One day, as he was walking along a country road on a fine spring morning, he felt happy and lazy. The sun was shining and the air was warm.

As he ambled along the road without a care in the world, he glanced up into the sky. Swooping between the white clouds was a solitary bird.

"I do believe that's a swallow!" exclaimed the man with delight. "They only fly here when summer is on the way. There must be many other swallows coming. That means that summer is almost here."

The man thought that he had solved his problems. If summer was coming, he would not need his coat. He could sell his coat and buy food with the money.

He did just that, selling his fine coat to the first person he met on the road.

But almost at once, things began to go wrong. The spring weather turned very cold, killing many birds and wild animals. The shivering man came across the swallow's frozen body on the ground.

"Because of you I sold my coat," he wailed. "Now I am freezing!"

Moral: *One swallow does not make a summer.*

A BOY BATHING

A boy thought that it would be fun to go for a swim in a river. His friends warned him that it was very deep, but he would not listen to them.

Soon after he had dived in, he found that he was out of his depth. He grew very frightened.

"Help me!" he cried. "I am drowning!"

A man happened to be walking with his dog along the bank of the river. He looked angrily at the poor boy.

"You silly lad!" he shouted. "Don't you know how dangerous that river is? You are a young fool!"

"Please sir," wailed the boy, feeling himself sinking, "if it's all the same to you, could you save me first and tell me off later?"

Moral: *We need to be helped, not scolded, when we are in*
trouble.

THE PIG AND THE SHEEP

A pig managed to get out of its sty. It ran away and joined a flock of sheep grazing in a field. The sheep made friends with the pig and allowed it to stay with them.

Then the farmer came along. When he saw the pig he picked it up and carried it off under his arm.

"I'll take you to the butcher, my lad," he told the animal.

At this the pig set up a dreadful squealing and wriggling as it tried to escape. The grazing sheep were amazed.

"What are you making such a fuss about?" one of them asked. "We don't make a fuss like that when the farmer carries us off."

"Perhaps you don't," squealed the pig. "He wants a lot more from me than he does from you. He wants you for your wool, but he wants me for bacon!"

Moral: *We should not make up our minds until we know the truth.*

133

THE FOX AND THE GRAPES

The fox came padding across the fields in the golden sunlight. His pointed ears were alert. He sniffed the air for any sign of danger. He was a fox and all men were against him.

At the edge of a vineyard he stopped. Thousands of tangled vines crept over high wooden frames. Hanging from the vines were great bunches of juicy grapes.

"I'll steal some before the owner comes," the fox decided.

He reached up and snapped at the nearest grapes. The bunch was too far above his head. Snarling with rage he backed off and leapt into the air, snapping with his great jaws.

He missed! Howling with rage, the fox tried again. For over an hour he ran and jumped, ran and jumped. He could not reach any of the grapes.

At last he gave up and slunk away. "I didn't want those grapes at all really," he muttered. "They were sour and useless!"

Moral: *Sometimes when we cannot get what we want, we pretend that we did not want it at all really.*

THE PRECIOUS GIFT

Once upon a time, there was a King who had three daughters.
One day, one of them would be queen. The King could not decide
which of them it should be, for they were all beautiful and they
were all clever.

"I must make up my mind somehow," he said. "I wonder what
I can do?" He thought, and he thought, and at last he made a
decision. "I will ask each of my daughters to bring me a gift,"
he said, "and the one who brings the most precious shall be
queen."

On the appointed day he summoned them to the throne room.

The eldest brought a silver bird in a silver cage, which sang when a key was wound.

"A truly beautiful gift," murmured the King.

The second daughter brought a robe of finest silk, trimmed with the softest fur.

"Another truly beautiful gift," murmured the King.

The third daughter brought a plain china bowl which was so small it nestled in the palm of her hand. The King held his breath as he lifted the lid. What precious gift would he find inside it? When the King saw what was in the tiny bowl his face went red, and then it went purple.

"How dare you!" he shouted. He jumped to his feet and threw the little bowl to the floor.

"How dare you insult me by bringing me common salt!"

"But . . . but . . ." The poor little princess tried to say something, but the King shouted and the more he shouted the more angry he became.

"Go!" he shouted. "Go! And never come back. Never! Never! NEVER!"

Of course he was sorry he had said what he did when his temper cooled down, but by then it was too late. The little princess had left the palace.

She wandered sadly until she came to an inn.

"Please let me stay here," she begged. "I have nowhere to go. I will work. I will do anything you ask."

The innkeeper did not know she was a princess or he would have given her his best room and waited on her himself. Instead he sent her down to the kitchen to help the cook.

The cook was a kindly woman. She taught the little princess all she knew about cooking. The princess was quick to learn and before long people were coming to the inn specially to taste her pies and to sample her soups and sauces. The kindly old cook was getting old and gradually the little princess did more and more of the cooking, until soon, she was doing it all.

Everyone who went to the inn talked for days afterwards about the delicious food eaten there, and it was only a matter of time before the King came to hear about the cook who could cook anything, and what was more, cook it perfectly.

"She must come to work in the palace kitchens," he said. "She is the best, and the King always has the best."

And so it was, that the King's own daughter, worked in the palace kitchens and cooked the King's meals, and no one, least of all the King, had any idea who she really was.

The day came when the King's eldest daughter was to be married. Such a hustle and a bustle there was in the palace kitchens. Any banquet is important, but a wedding banquet is the most important of all, especially when a princess is marrying a prince. The little princess, who was now the cook, worked hard and long to get everything prepared.

After the wedding the King and his guests sat down at the tables in the banqueting hall. The King clapped his hands.

"Let the banquet and the merry-making begin," he cried.

The pages and the footmen filed into the hall carrying silver platters piled high with the most delicious food it had ever been the King's privilege to see.

"What a wonderful cook you must have," said a visiting emperor.

The King felt so proud. And then, as was the custom, he lifted his fork and took the first bit of food. Everyone watched, and waited for the sign that they too could begin to eat. To their astonishment the King pulled a face and spat out the food. Princes and princesses, lords and ladies, footmen and pages, stared at the King with open mouths as he tried dish, after dish, scowling harder and harder with each mouthful he tasted. Suddenly he threw down his fork and in a voice like thunder, he shouted, "FETCH THE COOK!"

He looked so angry everyone trembled, even the visiting emperor, and he didn't frighten easily.

"What's wrong? . . . what's wrong? . . ." echoed in whispers round the hall.

The cook came and stood, with her head bowed, in front of the King, who by now was scarlet with rage.

"You have cooked the food without salt!" he roared. "The banquet is ruined! You have shamed me in front of my guests! How dare you forget something so important!"

"But I did not forget," said the cook, who was really a princess. The King was so astonished at a humble cook daring to answer him back he said nothing, and so she was able to continue.

"A long time ago, you banished a daughter because she gave you a gift of common salt . . ."

The King sat down with a bump on his chair. Yes, he did remember that. He had been sorry ever since. But how did the cook know about it? He looked at her closely. She lifted her head so that he could see her face, and smiled. The King jumped to his feet, scattering dishes with a clatter he did not hear.

"Daughter . . ." he cried. "It's you! Can you ever forgive me? You truly gave me a very precious gift and I was too foolish to know it."

Of course the princess forgave her father. And the banquet was not spoilt because she had arranged that only the King's food should be cooked without salt. There was more food already prepared for him in the kitchen.

And so the King and his daughter were reunited and the princess once again took her rightful place in the palace.

THE OXEN AND THE WAGON

Two oxen were pulling a loaded wagon along a road. It was very hard work. The road was full of holes. The wagon was heavy and hard to pull. The oxen had to strain every muscle to make the wagon move at all.

Behind them the wagon was making a great fuss, complaining all the time. Its wheels groaned and creaked.

Suddenly one of the oxen could no longer bear the dreadful noise being made by the wagon. He looked back over his aching shoulder and said, "What have you got to complain about? My brother and I are doing all the work!"

Moral: *They complain most who suffer least.*

THE HOUND AND THE LION

A hound decided to enter the jungle and see what he could find there. He had never been in the jungle before and did not know many of the animals who lived there. This did not worry him. Where he came from, he had been considered a great hunter. He had chased and killed many animals. He was sure that all the beasts of the jungle would be afraid of him.

Before very long he saw a lion walking ahead of him. This was the first lion the hound had ever seen. The thought did not worry the hound at all. He thought that he would soon catch the great beast.

For a time the hound followed the lion through the jungle. Then he broke into a trot and prepared to leap on the other beast.

Just as he reached the lion, the great animal turned and stared at the hound. Something warned the hound that the beast he was facing was stronger and fiercer than any he had ever met before.

For a moment the two animals stared at each other. Then the lion opened his mouth and roared.

The hound had never heard such a terrifying sound. The roar echoed among the trees. The hound discovered that he could not move. He stared at the savage teeth of the lion. He noticed the strength in the beast's shoulders. Then the hound turned and ran.

He raced through the jungle as fast as he could go, his heart thumping with fear. He had only one wish, and that was to put as much distance as possible between himself and the animal with the dreadful roar and the frightening teeth.

A fox who had been watching, laughed aloud and called after the vanishing hound:

"It didn't take much to make you run, my friend!"

142

Moral: *We should find out as much as possible about someone before coming into conflict with him.*

A MAN AND HIS SONS

Once there was a man who had five big sons. Instead of living together calmly and quietly, these sons were always quarrelling among themselves.

Their father grew tired of their constant bickering. He made up his mind to show them how silly they were.

He picked five sticks, each the same length, from the woodpile. Then he tied them together into a bundle. When this was done, he called his five sons to him. At first they did not hear him, because they were too busy arguing, but in the end they came.

"Listen to me!" shouted their father. "Take this bundle of sticks, and break it over your knee."

"I can do that easily," scoffed the eldest son.

He took the bundle and pulled it against his knee with all his force. No matter how hard he tried, he could not break the five sticks in the bundle.

"It can't be done," he growled at last.

"Of course it can," shouted his brothers. They all began arguing as to which of them should be the one to break the bundle. In the end they all tried in turn. Although their knees became sore, the bundle of sticks remained unbroken.

"Now let me show you how it can be done," said their father grimly.

He took the bundle of sticks from the others and untied the rope which held them together. Then he handed one stick to each of his five sons.

"Now, each of you break the stick in your hands," he ordered.

The sons did as they were told. Each stick cracked easily, like pieces of matchwood.

"What do you make of that?" their father asked them.

His sons looked puzzled, shrugging and making no answer. Their father sighed.

"Don't you see?" he explained patiently. "When a man stands alone, he can be broken as easily as one of those sticks. But when a man stands united with others nothing can break him."

Only then did his sons understand what their father had been trying to tell them, and they were all ashamed of themselves.

Moral: *United we stand, divided we fall.*

JORINDA AND JORINGEL

Once upon a time, there was a witch who lived in a castle in the middle of a dark and tangled wood. By day she read her magic books, but by night she changed herself into an owl and flew about the wood, ready to cast a spell on anyone who dared to get too close to her castle.

One day a boy and girl were walking in the wood. They had a wedding to plan and a lot to talk about, and they went deeper into the wood than they intended. Just as the sun was about to set, Joringel said, "We should turn for home . . . we are getting too close to the witch's castle." But it was already too late, for even as he spoke an owl flew from the trees and circled round them.

"Whoo! Whoo! Whoo!" it cried. The witch's spell had been cast. Joringel could not move and Jorinda had been turned into a little brown bird.

The owl flew into the middle of a bush. There was a rustle, and a moment later the old witch herself appeared. She caught the brown bird in a wicker cage and hurried away with it towards the castle. And though Joringel could see everything as it happened, he could do nothing to help Jorinda. He was rooted to the spot. And there he stayed, as still as a stone statue, until the old witch returned and removed the spell.

"Where is Jorinda? What have you done with her? Please bring her back to me," he begged. But the old witch was deaf to all his pleas.

"Go home . . ." she said. "Stop wasting my time."

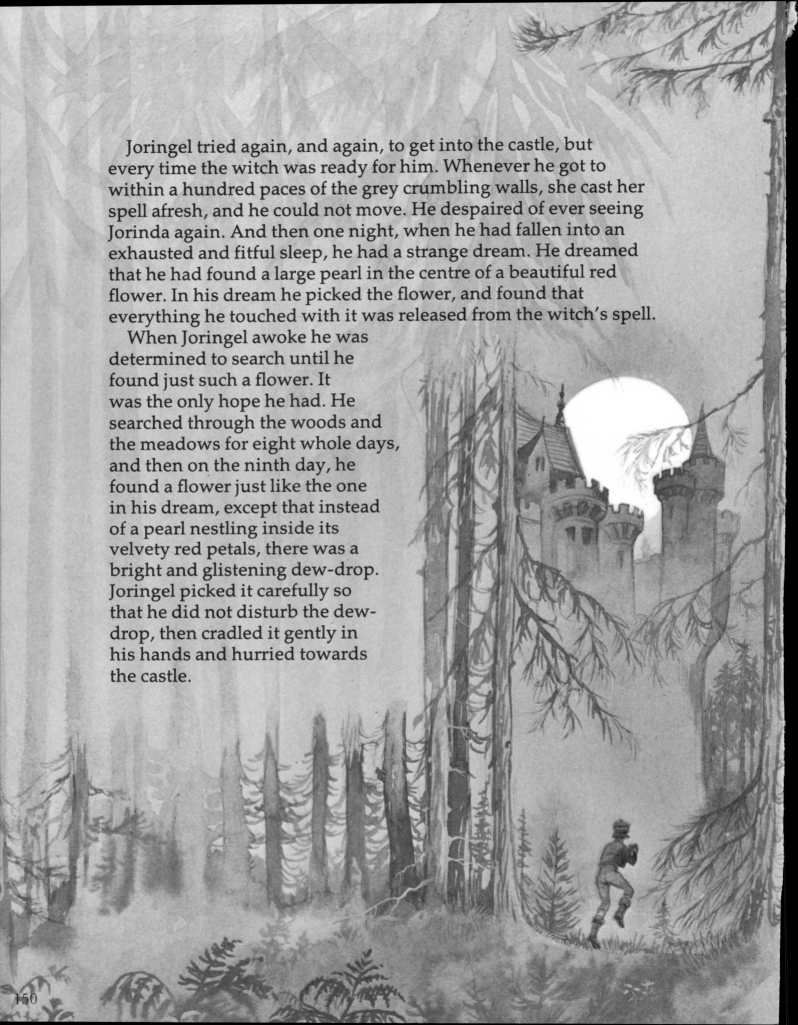

Joringel tried again, and again, to get into the castle, but every time the witch was ready for him. Whenever he got to within a hundred paces of the grey crumbling walls, she cast her spell afresh, and he could not move. He despaired of ever seeing Jorinda again. And then one night, when he had fallen into an exhausted and fitful sleep, he had a strange dream. He dreamed that he had found a large pearl in the centre of a beautiful red flower. In his dream he picked the flower, and found that everything he touched with it was released from the witch's spell.

When Joringel awoke he was determined to search until he found just such a flower. It was the only hope he had. He searched through the woods and the meadows for eight whole days, and then on the ninth day, he found a flower just like the one in his dream, except that instead of a pearl nestling inside its velvety red petals, there was a bright and glistening dew-drop. Joringel picked it carefully so that he did not disturb the dew-drop, then cradled it gently in his hands and hurried towards the castle.

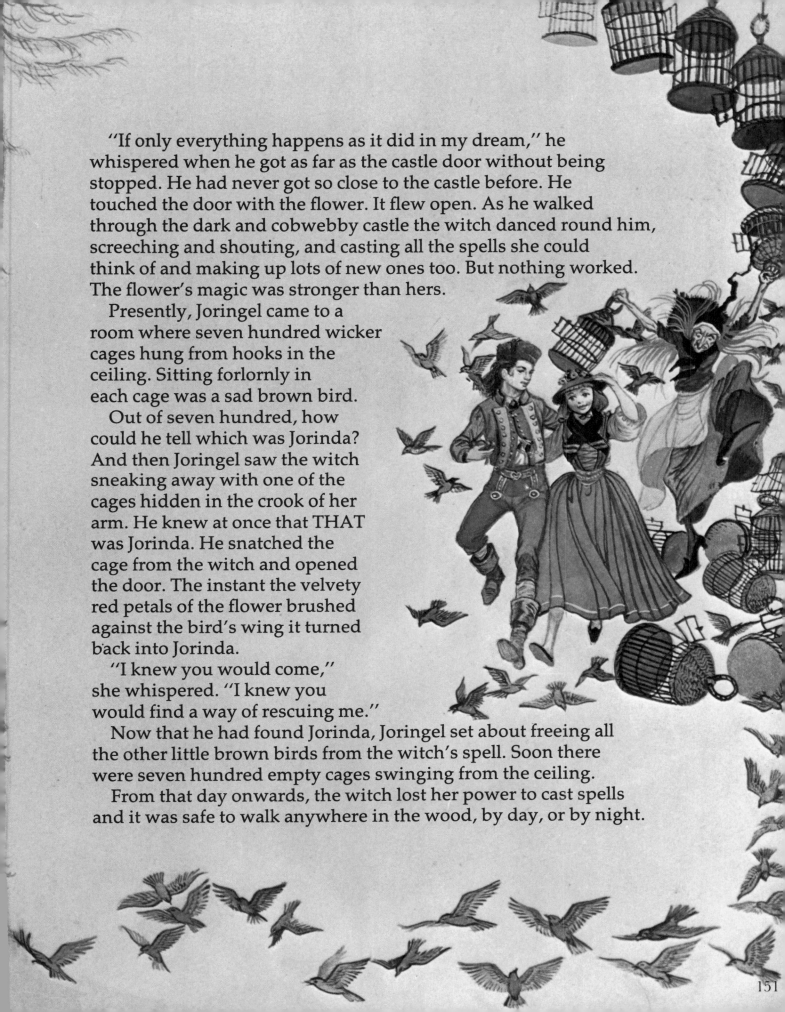

"If only everything happens as it did in my dream," he whispered when he got as far as the castle door without being stopped. He had never got so close to the castle before. He touched the door with the flower. It flew open. As he walked through the dark and cobwebby castle the witch danced round him, screeching and shouting, and casting all the spells she could think of and making up lots of new ones too. But nothing worked. The flower's magic was stronger than hers.

Presently, Joringel came to a room where seven hundred wicker cages hung from hooks in the ceiling. Sitting forlornly in each cage was a sad brown bird.

Out of seven hundred, how could he tell which was Jorinda? And then Joringel saw the witch sneaking away with one of the cages hidden in the crook of her arm. He knew at once that THAT was Jorinda. He snatched the cage from the witch and opened the door. The instant the velvety red petals of the flower brushed against the bird's wing it turned back into Jorinda.

"I knew you would come," she whispered. "I knew you would find a way of rescuing me."

Now that he had found Jorinda, Joringel set about freeing all the other little brown birds from the witch's spell. Soon there were seven hundred empty cages swinging from the ceiling.

From that day onwards, the witch lost her power to cast spells and it was safe to walk anywhere in the wood, by day, or by night.

THE SOLDIER AND HIS HORSE

Long ago there was a soldier who took great care of his horse. He knew that in battle his life might depend upon his steed. He always made sure that his mount was fed upon the best oats. He always gave him the cleanest water to drink. He made sure that his grooms polished the horse's sides until they shone. At night the soldier would never sleep, until he was sure that his horse was well-cared for and had a roof over its head.

In return the horse served its master well. It carried the soldier into battle and never flinched or turned away, no matter how fierce the fighting.

But then the war ended and the soldier rode back home. He put away his sword and his armour and became a farmer. He spent his days working in the fields.

In its turn the horse was also set to work on the farm. From dawn to dusk it toiled in the fields. It pulled a plough and did all the other hard jobs on the estates of its master.

Because there was no more fighting to be done, the soldier who was now a farmer no longer paid any attention to his steed. The horse was fed upon the poorest chaff. No one polished its coat and no one seemed to care where it slept at night.

Because of this neglect the horse grew thin and miserable. It was now a work-horse, not a warhorse.

Then one day the war broke out again. The farmer was asked to become a soldier once more. He answered this call. He put on his armour, took up his sword and gave orders that his horse should be brought in from the fields, its coat polished and its saddle put back on.

All this was done, and the soldier set off on his mount. He did not get very far. The years of neglect had made his horse thin and weak. It could not carry the weight of its master. Before long its knees buckled and it fell to the ground.

''You will have to travel on foot,'' it told the soldier. ''Years of hard work and bad food have turned me from a horse into a donkey. You cannot turn a donkey back into a horse at a moment's notice.''

Moral: *We must treat people properly if we expect their help.*

THE GOATHERD AND THE GOAT

Soon night would be falling. The goatherd wandered anxiously over the side of the mountain, rounding up all the goats in his charge. He had to get them all back to their pen at the farmhouse before it grew dark.

One by one the goats came to him as he called and whistled. The goatherd counted his charges. There was no doubt about it, one was still missing.

The man looked about him. To his relief he saw the missing goat in the distance. He shouted to the animal to come to him. The goat paid no attention.

Again and again the goatherd shouted and whistled. It was to no avail. The goat would not approach him. The man began to grow desperate. If he returned to the farm with one goat missing, the farmer would blame him.

Losing his temper, the goatherd picked up a stone and threw it at the animal. He did not mean to hurt it, but as it happened, the stone hit the goat on the head and broke the tip from one of its horns.

"Oh dear!" cried the goatherd, running towards the goat. "Please don't tell the farmer what I have done to your horn."

"You silly fellow," bleated the goat. "Can't you see that my broken horn will show what you have done to me, even if I don't tell the farmer?"

Moral: *It is no use trying to hide what cannot be hidden.*